THE
CONTINGENCY

PART ONE OF THE
CONTINGENCY WAR SERIES

G J OGDEN

ISBN-13: 978-1-9160426-3-6

Cover design by germancreative
Editing by S L Ogden

www.ogdenmedia.net

THE CONTINGENCY WAR SERIES

No-one comes in peace. Every being in the galaxy wants something, and is willing to take it by force...

READ THE OTHER BOOKS IN THE SERIES:

- The Contingency
- The Waystation Gambit
- Rise of Nimrod Fleet
- Earth's Last War

 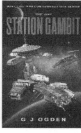  

ACKNOWLEDGEMENTS

Thanks to Sarah for her work assessing and editing this novel, and to those who subscribed to my newsletters and provided such valuable feedback.

And thanks, as always, to anyone who is reading this. It means a lot. If you enjoyed it, please help by leaving a review on Amazon and Goodreads to let other potential readers know what you think!

If you'd like updates on future novels by G J Ogden, please consider subscribing to the mailing list. Your details will be used to notify subscribers about upcoming books from this author, in addition to a hand-selected mix of book offers and giveaways from similar SFF authors.

http://subscribe.ogdenmedia.net

ONE

Casey Valera swiveled her pilot's chair towards Blake Meade, who had been asleep at his tactical console for fifteen minutes. Watching carefully for any signs of stirring she soundlessly slid the sequined purple sneaker off her right foot. She had waited just long enough for the ship's Tactical Specialist to drift off into a deep and comfortable sleep; any sooner and he would have been too easily roused from his regulation-breaking on-duty slumber.

Casey slid down in her chair to achieve some additional reach and lifted up her long leg, pointing her foot like a ballerina. Extending her leg towards Blake, she stretched out her yellow-varnished toes so that they just reached underneath his nose, which

1

wrinkled as her toe hovered over his top lip. She stifled a laugh and flexed her toes, maintaining a laser-precise distance from Blake's wiry black nose hairs as he snuffled and began to stir, forcing Casey to cover her mouth to keep from laughing out loud. She withdrew her foot an inch further from his face and waited for Blake to drop off fully again, before she pounced, pressing her big toe up against his nostrils, blocking them off completely. The operation was performed with the sort of dancer-like elegance that typified every movement Casey made. Her natural grace and style was one reason why she was perfect for the role of piloting a deep-space recon ship. Unable to breathe, Blake coughed and spluttered and woke suddenly, gasping for breath. His head turned on a swivel and his guard was raised as if he was expecting a fight, despite there being only four people on the entire ship, which was thousands of light years from Earth.

"What the hell?!" he shouted, rubbing his nose. "Casey, was that you again?"

Casey had swiftly returned to her normal sitting position during the confusion of Blake's rude awakening. She had swiveled her chair back to face the main viewport again, and was pretending to innocently survey her instruments when Blake leveled the accusation at her.

"Was what me?" she asked, shooting Blake a well-rehearsed feigned look of shocked surprise.

Then her eyes narrowed, and she threw an accusation of her own right back at him, "Blakey... have you been sleeping on duty again?"

Blake Meade ruffled his short-cropped brown hair and then rubbed his eyes. "Cut out the act, Casey, I know it was you. That better not have been your stinkin' foot again."

Casey snorted a laugh, but then attempted to disguise it as a cough, which would have fooled no-one, especially not the naturally observant TacSpec crew member.

"I haven't the faintest idea what you mean," said Casey, now switching to her 'affronted' act. "You should be more worried about the Cap finding you snoozing on the job, and spend less time focusing on my toes."

Blake glanced down and saw that one of Casey's non-regulation sequined purple sneakers was resting by the side of her bare right foot, while the other was still worn. His lips curled into a smile. *Gotcha, bang to rights...* he thought.

"It's funny you should mention your toes, 'cause I'm damn sure the Cap don't allow snot-yellow toe-nails. Oh, and by the way, you're missin' one of those ugly purple sneakers."

Casey kept her eyes focused on the panels in front of her, but searched around with her foot, eventually finding the errant sneaker and slipping it back on.

"The Cap likes my toenails, I'll have you know."

Blake laughed. "No he don't. That cheerless bastard only likes two things – the mission, and staring at Satomi's ass."

Casey laughed and smiled at him, and Blake returned the smile with equal warmth. Casey was about the only thing that had made the near four years of their mission tolerable for him. And despite her annoying tendency to prank him, if it hadn't been for her joyous laugh filling their small air-filled tub in the middle of the nothingness, he'd probably have gone mad. Her laugh was blissful, like having your brain massaged with soundwaves.

"Don't knock it, can you imagine how grumpy he'd be out here without her to distract his attention away from duty, duty, duty?"

"Yeah, you're right," yawned Blake. "That's prob'ly why she's here in the first place. Y'know, all that personality-matching mumbo jumbo they make us go through is only so we don't end up killin' each other before the four years is up."

Casey beamed at him and made a heart symbol with her hands. "Aww, that must mean we were always destined to be bosom pals then?"

"Not if you keep stickin' your stinkin' toes up my nose!"

They both burst into giggles and Blake drank in the sound of her laughter again. Wiping a mirth-induced tear from his eye, Blake added, "Where are those two anyhow? Still in the lab, findin' us another pointless corner of the galaxy to search?"

Casey shot him a reproaching look. "Come on Blakey, we only have two more weeks to go and then we're done. Besides, I like it out here."

Blake shook his head. "You must be the only pilot in all of Earth Fleet that actually likes flying deep space recon missions."

Casey raised her legs and rested them gracefully on the top of the pilot's console. The purple sequins on her sneakers glistened, reflecting the many glowing screens, dials and indicators that adorned her station. "Of course I do, what's not to love? It's peaceful out here. There's a beauty to it, know what I mean?"

Blake grunted. "No. There ain't no beauty out here, just a whole lotta nothin'. We've been to over thirty systems and it's the same every time; nothin', nothin', and more damn nothin'."

"Then why did you volunteer, Mr. Grumpy?"

Blake cocked an eyebrow at the quirky young pilot. "The pay, of course, dummy, same as every other sane and normal person." He yawned again and rested his hands behind his head, while relaxing back in his chair. "I get ten years' worth of regular TacSpec pay for just four years spent driftin' around in the ass-end of the galaxy, searchin' for ghosts."

"They could still be out here, you know."

"You don't believe that any more than I do," said

Blake, with a dismissive waft of his hand. "Believe me, I'd welcome nothin' more than an opportunity to take out the last dregs of the Hedalt Empire. But the fact is the fleet mopped up all the outposts within a few years of nuking their home world. Those that fled didn't get far, either. The ugly bastards aren't suited for space travel, not like us."

When Casey remained silent, Blake glanced across and saw that, for the first time since she had woken him up by shoving a toe up his nose, her normally joyous, vibrant glow was missing. He studied her face, noting that her freckle-covered cheeks were no longer raised up, so that even her eyes weren't smiling. Blake had spent enough time with Casey Valera over the last four years to know the cause of her sudden melancholy.

"Hey, it was us or them, Casey, and they started it," said Blake balling his hands together in his lap and sitting more upright. "We did what we had to do to survive. There ain't nothin' more to it than that."

Casey stared blankly out through the viewport and into the void of space. "I know, Blake, it's just sad that's all. I know they invaded our system, and I know they killed billions, but still..." she hesitated.

"Still what?"

"Extermination just seems a little extreme..."

Blake laughed, and Casey shot him a dirty look. "Don't laugh at me, you brute. We're not all cold-hearted beasts like you!"

"You do realize that extermination is why we're out here, Casey? We're not out here scourin' the galaxy for any remaining Hedalt outposts just so we can rock up and say, 'Hey! Sorry we nuked your planet and wiped out your species!' and invite them out for a beer to make up for it."

"I don't want to nuke them or have a beer with them; I'm just out here because I like flying," said Casey, with some of the vibrancy returning to her cheeks.

"Yeah, well don't you worry 'bout it, Casey, they're long dead, like I said," Blake replied, relaxing again now that Casey seemed to be returning to her usual self. "And I ain't gonna shed a tear if we do find a colony and have to turn it to rubble. They did the same to us; they'd do it again, given half a chance. It's just nature, is all. Survival of the strongest."

"You TacSpecs are all the same; animals. I should put a collar on you."

Blake smirked and winked at Casey. "That's not really my kind of scene, but thanks for the offer, all the same."

Casey shook her head, trying her hardest to look deeply disappointed in him, but she was unable to hide a thin smile. "I don't know how I ever got matched with you."

"Just lucky, I guess."

The door to the bridge slid open and Captain Taylor Ray walked in, followed shortly by the ship's

Technical Specialist, Satomi Rose.

"Unless you plan on flying this ship with your feet," Taylor began, with a sort of affable sternness, "can you please take them off the console, Casey."

Casey tilted her head backwards and smiled at Taylor, looking at him upside down. "I graduated top of my academy class in foot flying, Cap."

Taylor rolled his eyes and continued onto the bridge, stopping in the center of the deck, as Casey swiveled her chair around to face him, whipping her legs off the console with the same grace with which she'd placed them there earlier. Taylor noticed the sparkling purple sneakers twinkling under the harsh lights of the bridge and shook his head again. "I guess I should be grateful that you're wearing shoes at all..."

"They're sneakers Cap, and I knew you'd like them!" said Casey, beaming at him.

Blake also spun his chair around to face his fellow crew members, and got straight to the point. "We got a new destination yet, Cap? Casey over here is on the verge of falling asleep." Casey glowered at him, but he pretended not to notice.

"That's actually what I'm here to tell you," said Taylor, "and I'm sorry, the answer is no, not yet. We're still awaiting some updated information from the CoreNet, before we can make a final decision."

Satomi now spoke up. "The problem is that we've travelled so far from the closest super-luminal transceiver that it's taking a while for the data to work its way through the Fabric."

'The Fabric' was the more colloquial term for the sub-layer of space accessed by a vast network of nodes that stretched out across the galaxy. Earth Fleet believed them to have been built by the Hedalt, countless thousands of years ago. Each node, or 'super-luminal transceiver' to give them their official designation, was connected to the others through engineered wormholes called threads. Together, it created a patchwork quilt of connected super-luminal transceivers that spanned most of the known galaxy, hence the name, the Fabric. The Fabric also acted as a super-highway for faster-than-light navigation. It made it possible to jump extremely long distances from node to node, like express lines between railway stations. The alternative was to spend hours or sometimes days computing blind jumps, which had a far more limited range.

The reactions of Casey and Blake to Taylor's news were polar opposites of each other. Casey continued to beam back at the Captain, happy for the delay, because it meant more hours floating serenely in the expanse of space. Meanwhile, Blake's shoulders slumped and his head dropped low, knowing it would likely be at least another day or two before anything remotely interesting happened on the ship.

"The Captain and I have been hard at work crunching the numbers," continued Satomi, while walking briskly over to her mission operations console on the left of the bridge. Taylor followed her and while his back was turned, Blake smirked and tapped a quick private message to Casey using the communication system built into the arm of his chair. 'Hard at work crunching each other, more like...'

He looked over to Casey, eagerly anticipating her reaction, and watched as she read the message, following the line of her mouth as it curled upward. She glanced back at him, eyebrows raised, and mouthed the words, "That doesn't even make sense..." But, Casey had expected nothing less, and perversely this was why she'd found it amusing. From the countless whispered words and private messages Blake had sent over the course of four years in deep space, one thing she had learned with absolute certainly was that Blake was terrible at innuendo.

"Our current location puts us several parsecs beyond the furthest deep space recon vessel ever to visit this part of the Fabric," Satomi went on, oblivious to the antics behind her. "But I believe there are some good prospects within our safe blind jump range. I'm just waiting for the computer to process the final data so that we can select the ideal system." She tapped away at the console, confirming some final numbers, before turning back to face the others. "We only have time for one more jump, before heading home, so I want to make it a good one."

Taylor turned around and fixed his gaze directly at Blake. "And no, before you ask, Tactical Specialist Meade, we're not just going to sit out here and watch the clock run down. We have a mission to perform."

"Wouldn't have it any other way, Cap!" said Blake, lying. "I just hope we see some action before I get to lounge on my fat ass back home and drink away my not inconsiderable bounty."

"That's the spirit, Blake!" said Taylor, with enthusiasm, but then he decided he needed to clarify his statement. "I mean about seeing some action, not drinking away all your pay."

"The way he drinks, he'll be broke again in less than a month," said Casey, then she smiled at Blake and added, "then he'll be back out here with me again, won't you Blakey?"

Blake laughed. "I'd rather work on the garbage scows. Dumpin' trash into the sun is more appealin' than havin' your toes stuck up my nose."

Taylor considered asking Blake to clarify exactly what he meant by that statement, but then thought better of it. Blake and Casey often spoke a language that only they understood.

Satomi shut her eyes and massaged the back of her neck. She could tolerate the back-and-forth between Blake and Casey for short bursts, and even enjoyed it and joined in on occasions, but she was tired and not currently in the mood for their silliness. "I suggest we all turn in for the night; it will be at least another five hours before the computer has finished processing." Then she turned to Taylor and added, apologetically, "With your approval, of course, Captain."

"Good idea, Satomi; I don't know about the rest of you, but I'm beat."

Blake glanced over to Casey and waggled his eyebrows at her suggestively. Casey just mouthed back the words, "That also doesn't make any sense..."

Remarkably neither Taylor nor Satomi appeared to spot the exchange.

"Let's reconvene on the bridge at zero six hundred," continued Taylor. "Casey, please rig the ship for automatic."

"Aye, aye, Captain Taylor Ray," chirped Casey, breezily. She always used his full rank and title when responding to a direct order; it was another quirk about her that Blake loved.

Taylor swept off the bridge, followed a few seconds behind by Satomi, who called out, "See you guys in the morning..." before heading through the door, without waiting for a reply.

Casey sprang into action, turning the mundane and highly procedural task of adjusting dials and flipping switches to configure the ship for automatic running while they slept into an almost hypnotically expressive form of performance art.

Blake stood up and stretched, which caused him to inadvertently break wind. "Oops, sorry 'bout that..." he said, though his amused expression suggested his apology was far from genuine.

"I take it back, you're worse than an animal!" cried Casey. "Go on, get off my bridge."

"Yes, ma'am. Aren't you comin'?"

"Not yet."

Blake smiled. Casey often sat on the bridge alone after the others had retired, sometimes for hours, and she was always the last to go to sleep. For someone who loved being with people – and who was so easy to get along with – her frequent desire for solitude was one of the many little idiosyncrasies that made her so special, at least to Blake.

"Okay then, Casey, I'll see you in the morning."

"Night, night, Blakey!" Casey called out, waving a hand above her head as he left, but not taking her eyes off the blackness of space outside the viewport.

Casey listened to Blake's heavy boots clump away and waited for the bridge door to hiss open and then slide shut again, before relaxing back in the chair and swinging her feet up and onto the console again. She reached into her jacket pocket and pulled out a heavily worn packet of candies, taking out and unwrapping a single, bullet-shaped red mint and popping it into her mouth, before closing the pack and placing it back in her pocket again. Her primary status console chimed softly and flashed up a message. She leant forward to read it, sucking gently on the mint.

"What have we here?" she said out loud, reading the data on the screen.

Signal detected

Source: [Calculating, ETA 4:23:18]

Origin: Hedalt - probability 18.4% [calculating]

"Well, I'll be damned," said Casey, letting out a long, low whistle. Returning her sequined sneakers to the deck, she tapped a command into the keypad on her chair, and then calmly waited for the response, savoring the flavor of the candy, which was part of her night-time ritual.

Advise protocol. Should I alert Captain?

...

...

Negative: Await source calculation

Origin probability should exceed 50%

"You're the boss," said Casey, entering a command to activate the crew alarm if the origin probability reached fifty per cent. "I bet it's just another false reading, anyway," she commented to herself, while maneuvering the mint under her tongue. She finished executing the command and slumped back down in the chair, lifting her sequined sneakers back onto the console. Then she closed her

14

eyes and flicked the mint back into the center of her tongue, before pressing it gently to the roof of her mouth. Unseen to her, the status console updated again.

Signal detected
Source: [Calculating, ETA 4:20:23]
Origin: Hedalt - probability 19.7% [rising]

TWO

Captain Taylor Ray awoke with a start to the sound of the mission alert siren ringing in his ears. He shielded his eyes against the pulsating warning lights in his cabin, which flashed in a vibrant red, causing his head to throb in time. He groaned and pushed himself into a sitting position, which only made his head feel worse. While he had been perfectly fine before going to bed, he now felt terrible, as if he'd drunk half a bottle of bourbon the night before, after three rounds of sparring with Blake. Touching the control panel next to the bed he croaked, "Cancel alert."

The piercing sound ceased and the cabin lights switched to a bright daylight-white, which did nothing to alleviate the thumping in his head. He touched the control panel again and added, "And lower the light level by thirty percent." The lights responded, and mercifully Taylor felt some of the discomfort ease off too.

He glanced over at the clock, which read 04:38, and groaned again. There was a knock at the door, *thud, thud, thud*. The knock wasn't especially hard, but it still felt like the visitor was rapping their knuckles directly on his brain.

"Come in..."

The door slid open to reveal Technical Specialist Satomi Rose, softly silhouetted by the brighter strip lights in the corridor behind her.

"Hell, you look like how I feel," Taylor said, noting Satomi's pained expression.

"What? I'm just a little disoriented, that's all," replied Satomi, who immediately went to straighten her hair, despite it being tied in a ponytail. "I was in a deep sleep when the alert..."

"Relax, Satomi, I'm joking," said Taylor, realizing that he'd offended her and attempting to dig himself out of the hole he had dug. "Well, at least about how you look, anyway. My head feels worse than it did the morning after my academy graduation ball. I didn't think that was possible."

The apology, though heavily disguised, was good enough for Satomi, and she felt less self-conscious. "Do you want me to get you some pain killers? Or, perhaps, hair of the dog?"

Taylor stood up and had to steady himself against the cabin wall to keep from falling over again. It was like an inner-ear imbalance combined with a furious hangover, and he had to stand perfectly still and breathe slowly and deliberately to stop from throwing up.

"I wish I could say that this was the result of drinking too much," said Taylor, between deep breaths, "but getting a hangover without actually having been drunk is like being told, 'we're not compatible' before you've even been on a date."

"I don't really go on dates, Captain," said Satomi, missing the point entirely.

Taylor frowned, but this only made his head hurt more and he squeezed his eyes shut.

"Are you sure you're alright, Taylor?" said Satomi. Taylor couldn't help but notice that she'd switched from 'Captain' to 'Taylor', which she always did when she was genuinely concerned about him. Even though he was her Captain, four years cooped up on a ship with only four people had meant that even his normally robust standards about protocol had slipped. He and Satomi had been a strong match in the personality profiling tests, and despite their efforts to retain a professional detachment, it was almost inevitable that they had become close. But it was a closeness in a guarded and awkward kind of way, like a couple of introverted teenagers.

Strangely, a few seconds after Satomi had asked if Taylor was okay, the nausea subsided as quickly as it had come on, and Taylor felt considerably better. Even his headache had eased substantially. He slipped on his shoes, smoothed the creases from his uniform, and stepped over to the door.

"Yes, I'm fine," said Taylor. "It's like you said; just a bit of a rude awakening from a deep sleep, that's all. I feel okay now."

Satomi stroked his arm and smiled at him. "Good, you had me worried there for a minute. We can't have the Captain getting sick when we're over twenty thousand light years away from Earth."

The figure startled Taylor; he had only been counting jump distances from their previous locations, rather than their total distance from home. "Hell, are we really that far out? When you say it out loud it sounds unbelievable."

"Yes sir, and we're about to head out even further," said Satomi, ominously. "Though not that much further, relatively speaking."

"You found something?"

"I'm not one hundred percent sure yet, but I think so."

Taylor massaged his stubbled chin and then ran his hand through his hair. Though his headache and nausea had subsided, he still felt a little strange, but he couldn't quite put his finger on why. It was like he'd walked into a door a few hours earlier and was still mildly concussed.

"It would be just our luck to find something with only two weeks left to run," said Taylor. He wasn't normally a pessimist, but the weariness of his current condition added to four years in deep space had dented his usual optimistic outlook.

"I think I've been lucky to have you as my Captain," said Satomi, holding her hands in front of her and gently rubbing her knuckles. "I just wanted to say that, before this is all over."

Taylor's eyes widened. Was this merely professional admiration, he wondered, or was it Satomi's back-to-front way of trying to tell him something? He never was any good at reading the signals, and this occasion was no different.

"Well, thanks, Satomi," said Taylor, allowing the confusion fogging his mind to color his words, making them sound artificial and bordering on insincere. *Thanks, Satomi? Damn it, Taylor, is that really the best you can do?*

Satomi smiled awkwardly and then stepped further out into the corridor, looking anywhere but at Taylor. "Anyway, the others will be assembling on the bridge now, so we can run through the detailed analysis together."

And, just like that, the moment is gone. Well played, Captain... Taylor admonished himself, and then cursed the fact he'd woken up feeling so groggy. Perhaps if his mind had been sharper, his response would have been keener too. He smiled at Satomi and almost considered apologizing, but thought better of it; he'd likely just end up digging himself into another hole. Instead, he said, "Okay, Satomi, lead the way..." He gestured for her to move out ahead, which she did, still careful not to meet his eyes.

They walked together in silence along the wide central corridor of their Nimrod-class deep space recon cruiser towards the bridge, passing the dining hall and other living quarters of the mid-sized vessel. For near-Earth duties, a ship of its size would have been crewed by at least a dozen, but for deep space recon missions, or DSRs for short, Earth Fleet had deemed it prudent to afford the extra space of the Nimrod-class to a four-person crew in order to prevent cabin fever. Early DSR missions that had used smaller ships had been fraught with problems, mainly due to the crew simply driving each other crazy. Taylor had initially thought the size of the Nimrod-class to be excessive, but after just a few months in space, he'd come to understand the logic behind the decision. He also welcomed the ability to get away from the others, if only for a short time. It was known as 'getting some air' in Earth Fleet lingo.

Besides, after the war with the Hedalt had

ended, there was no shortage of Nimrod-class cruisers in circulation, and it made sense to use them instead of mothballing them or tearing them down for parts and scrap. To Taylor that would have been a tragedy; these stalwart ships had played just as much of a part in saving the fate of humanity as their crews had, and they deserved respect too.

However, despite occasionally needing to 'get some air' the reality was that his four-person crew spent almost all their time together, usually happily. This was down to careful and detailed personality matching, which was introduced as a compulsory element of DSR crew selection shortly after the failures of early DSR missions had highlighted interpersonal issues as a major factor. In one case study, which was compulsory viewing for DSR volunteers to hammer home the importance of taking the test seriously, a ship's TacSpec crew member had actually killed the Captain. But, thanks to the careful matching process, Taylor was confident that his own TacSpec officer would not resort to similarly homicidal ways. Sure, Blake would sometimes shoot him murderous glances, but the reality was he would never harm one of the crew, which Taylor was very glad of indeed, given Blake's proficiency for violence. In fact, Blake was like everyone's tough bigger brother; he'd not hesitate to step in and fight for them all, no holds barred.

The same was true of the others too. Because of the personality matching, it was rare for serious disagreements to occur amongst his crew. They were in essence like one family.

Four years was still a long time to spend in each other's pockets, though, and it was only natural that tempers could become frayed from time to time, even amongst the most well-matched crews. It was during these times that the ability to just get lost in some disused part of the ship was welcome. DSR regulations permitted, and even encouraged, crew members to give themselves this head space, for as long as they needed it. After all, with only four crew, each relying on the other, a serious relationship issue – or the murder of a crew member – could jeopardize not only the mission, but all of their lives.

Satomi led them through the door, which swished open automatically, and onto the bridge, where Casey and Blake were already waiting. Casey was propped up against the back of her pilot's chair shielding her eyes against the lights, while Blake was slumped in his seat at the tactical station, massaging his temples.

"You guys too?" said Taylor, recognizing their symptoms as being remarkably like his own only a few minutes earlier. "Don't tell me; headache, nausea, disorientation, sensitivity to light?"

"Yeah, how'd you know?" said Blake. "I feel like I've had my ass kicked by a bottle of Tequila."

"You always were a lightweight," quipped Casey. "But, if I'm honest, I feel kinda the same way. I don't even remember getting into my bed last night."

"That's 'cause you tried to get into mine," Blake teased, "but, don't worry, I was a gentleman and kicked your sorry ass out again."

"You should be so lucky!"

Taylor raised a hand. "Okay you two, that's enough." How they could still manage to tease each other while both feeling as rough as he'd felt moments earlier was beyond him, but he was in no mood for it. "Don't worry about the headache, it will pass." He spoke confidently, seeking to offer reassurance, though the fact that all four of them had woken up with the same symptoms was now weighing heavily on his mind. "But, just to be sure, I want each of you to run a personal medical and feed the results into the computer by zero eight hundred, is that understood?"

Satomi and Blake nodded and acknowledged the order dutifully with a 'yes sir', while Casey replied in her customary manner.

"That includes me too," added Taylor, who was as eager to set his own mind at rest as he was to ensure his crew was fit and healthy. Sickness was one of the biggest dangers facing DSR missions. "Also, Satomi, please run a check on the air filtration systems and do a scan for anything that might be harmful; you know, alien bugs and that sort of thing."

"Yes Captain, scanning for 'alien bugs and that sort of thing' is one of my specialties..." she replied, smirking. She loved how awkward and clumsy-sounding the Captain got when talking about anything even remotely scientific. Then she noticed he was scowling at her, and decided to add an addendum, in a more professional tone, "I'll get on it directly after the briefing, Captain."

Taylor's concerns over the status of his crew's health had distracted him from the real reason they had all assembled in the first place. "Right, of course, the briefing," he said, clicking his fingers. "Well let's see what's so important that it meant waking us all up in the middle of the night." He nodded to Satomi and she moved over to the mission ops console and transferred the data to the main viewport so that everyone could see it.

"I know we're all feeling a little worse for wear, so I'll keep this brief and to the point," Satomi began.

"Great, then I can go back to bed..." Blake chimed in, but Satomi ignored him.

"We have detected a possible Hedalt signal..."

Satomi's statement immediately silenced Blake, who straighten up in his seat and began to rub his knuckles eagerly.

"My early analysis of the deep scan data puts the confidence level currently at fifty-three percent and still rising," Satomi continued, aware that she now had Blake's complete and undivided attention.

"Aw, c'mon, Satomi, that's borderline at best," said Blake, now feeling even more like he'd been cheated out of sleep for no good reason.

"True, but mission protocol states we have to investigate," said Satomi, glancing over to Taylor, hoping he would back her up.

He did. "Satomi is right."

Blake threw his hands up. "Can't we at least check with Earth Fleet command first? We're two weeks out from the end of our tour, for crying out loud!"

"We already know the answer," Taylor cut in, asserting control. "It doesn't matter if there are two weeks left on our tour or two hours; DSR mission rules say we go, so we go." Blake scowled, but remained silent. "They're not going to cut us any slack just because we're close to the end of our four years, and you know it," he continued, addressing Blake directly. Then Taylor's stiff stance and tight shoulders relaxed a little, as did the tone of his voice. "Besides, I thought you were eager to see some action before we head back?"

Blake groaned. "What I'm eager for is a couple

more hours of sleep. But, whatever, fine, one for the road, eh?"

Taylor glanced back at Satomi and nodded, indicating for her to continue the briefing.

"The signal origin is in a system that's quite far from our current position, but just within our safe blind-jump range, so I'm sure Casey can make it." Casey threw up a casual salute and winked at Satomi. "It's a system in a cluster of stars in the Scutum-Crux arm, close to where the arm intersects with the galactic long bar," continued Satomi, highlighting the system on a galactic map displayed on the viewport. "It's uncharted and no other DSR has been to this region, so it's worth checking out."

"The Scrotum-Crotch what-now?" said Blake, being deliberately facetious. "Though, I like the sound of a long bar; I could *really* do with finding one of those right now..."

Casey laughed. "Don't worry, Blakey, Casey's driving and she knows the way!"

Taylor stepped forward towards Blake, conscious that his playful protests were a prelude to a more deep-rooted resentment of the mission. Blake was the very definition of a 'glass half-empty' personality; if there was anything negative to highlight in any situation, Blake would be sure to point it out.

"Look, it's probably nothing, like it was

nothing the last thirty-odd times we've done this," Taylor said, addressing the room, but locking eyes on Blake specifically. "So let's just jump out there, confirm it's another ghost, and then we can all go home. Deal?"

Blake scrunched his nose up and sniffed dismissively. "Okay, Cap, you're the boss."

"Yes, I am," said Taylor, stiffly, and then he turned to Casey. "Satomi has already computed the course and sent the co-ordinates and calculations to the nav computer, so how soon can you make the jump?"

"Just give me one moment, Cap..." said Casey, almost singing the words, and then she pirouetted around into her pilot's chair and began another intricate ballet of button tapping and switch flipping. A few moments later, she swiveled her chair back around to face Taylor, cheeks raised high and eyes smiling. "Co-ordinates and jump program locked in, Cap. And the jump engines are charged and ready; I took the liberty of cycling them up as soon as I heard the words, 'Satomi is right' come out of your mouth." Her eyes twinkled over to Satomi, who was already waiting in position in her mission ops chair.

"But, I'm always right..." said Satomi, smiling back at Casey.

Taylor stepped over to his command chair in the center of the bridge and planted himself purposefully in the seat. "Okay, so I guess it's 'once more unto the breach, dear friends' then..."

"There he goes, quotin' Dickens again..." said Blake. He knew full well it wasn't a Dickens quote, but he also knew that Satomi would take the bait.

"For the one hundredth time, Blake, it's Shakespeare, not Dickens!" Satomi called over, sinking her teeth into the hook.

Taylor smiled and shot Blake a knowing look. For all his complaining, Blake loved this part of the mission. And so did Taylor.

"Okay, Casey, whenever you're ready, make the jump."

"Aye, aye, Captain Taylor Ray..."

THREE

The rising energy of the jump engines started to penetrate the bridge. It saturated the air with a low, pulsating whine that could be felt through the deck plates and through the arms of Taylor's chair, which he was gripping tightly, as if he was about to accelerate down a huge dip on a roller-coaster. He'd completed countless jumps before, including over thirty as Captain of his current Nimrod-class cruiser, but he had never become used to it, and never liked it. The best way he could describe it to his friends who had never experienced faster-than-light extra-solar travel was that it felt like being so drunk that the room spun around you, followed by the sensation of the world collapsing, as if your whole existence was a pop-up book that had just been slammed shut into darkness and nothingness. For an agonizing moment it was like being dead, but paradoxically aware that you were dead, until suddenly the book was opened again on a new page, popping you back into existence in a different part of the galaxy.

Casey spun around in her chair to face him, wearing a childlike grin of excitement, as if it was Christmas Day morning. Unsurprisingly, Casey loved making blind jumps, just as she adored anything and everything to do with space flight.

"Jumping in five...

...F o u r

...T h r e e

. . . T   w   o

. . . O   n   e

Casey started spinning around in her chair again, but Taylor had already pressed his eyes shut; he found it helped, or at least that's what he told himself. And then he too was spinning, but it was a swirling vortex in his mind, rather than the motion of his chair, which remained fixed to the spot. He gripped the arms of the chair more tightly as the feeling of being squashed out of existence pressed in on him, until he could feel absolutely nothing, and all that remained of Taylor Ray was disembodied, conscious thought. He was somehow still deeply aware of Satomi Rose, as if she was inside his mind with him. And he could still sense Casey Valera and Blake Meade too, in the same way that you can sense a person standing near you, despite not being able to see them. And then suddenly the universe exploded back into life and he could again feel the soft fabric on the arm of his command chair and taste the air filling his lungs. He opened his eyes to see Casey Valera still spinning around in the pilot's chair, purple sneakers sparkling in the warm light that filtered through the viewport from the new red sun that burned at the heart of another unexplored system.

Casey stopped spinning for just long enough to read the jump status report. "Jump complete, El Capitan. Engines standing down... All systems nominal." She spun around a full three hundred sixty degrees, before stopping the chair to face Taylor again. "Shall we knock and see who's home?"

Taylor pushed himself out of his seat, which suddenly felt very claustrophobic, and glanced over to Satomi. "Let's see if Satomi can find us a door to knock on first, shall we?"

Satomi was already out of her chair and flitting between the various different consoles on the mission operations station. "I'm scanning the system now, though it may take a while."

Blake yawned and slumped down in his seat. "Does that mean I can go back to bed?"

One of the mission ops consoles bleeped and

Satomi checked it urgently. A few seconds later she turned to Blake and smiled. "Sorry, but I'm afraid you'll just have to make do with a strong coffee."

Taylor hurried over to Satomi's side, suddenly alert. "You managed to find something already?"

"Yes, there's a weak signal coming from the fourth planet in the system. The planet is inside the Goldilocks Zone, although judging by the surface temperatures, I doubt it's still habitable now."

"Can you confirm that the signal is definitely Hedalt in origin?" added Taylor. He wasn't concerned with whether the planet was or ever had been habitable; confirming the signal was all that mattered.

Satomi didn't answer and instead continued to study the information that was flooding onto the many different screens on her console, each of which was casting chaotic dark green patterns across her face.

"Satomi, is it an active Hedalt signal or another ghost?" Taylor asked again, this time more impatiently and, although his voice was controlled, he could feel his heart starting to race.

Several more tense seconds passed without a response, and then Satomi stepped back from the console and pressed her hands to her hips, "I can't be certain from this range, Captain. It could just be an old outpost that's still putting out a ghost signal into the CoreNet, or it could be a live colony. The readings are inconclusive; we need to get closer."

Taylor nodded, took a long breath to calm his nerves, and then he marched briskly back to his command chair in the center of the bridge, filled with vigor and purpose.

"Casey, take us into orbit around the fourth planet in the system, sharply," he ordered, resting his arms on the back of his chair. He was still too wired to sit down again.

Casey smiled and threw up a salute, before spinning back to face the controls, "Aye, aye, Captain Taylor Ray."

Blake groaned, loudly and obviously, intending everyone to hear, "Did ya have to say, 'sharply', Cap?" complained Blake, burying himself securely into the recesses of his chair, more for show than out of necessity.

Casey glanced at him and winked, "Buckle up, Blakey."

Blake scowled, "Yeah, that'd be great. Problem is these damn chairs don't have seat buckles..."

FOUR

Out of the hundreds of thousands of people enrolled in Earth Fleet, only a tiny proportion were suited to DSR missions, and an even tinier proportion still were Captain material. To be suited for DSR, you had to be able to live in near-solitude, moving from system to system, spending weeks on mundane duties with no prospect of returning, and then immediately be able to 'switch on' when the mission demanded it. Paradoxically, DSR Captains had to be contented loners, but also naturally gregarious and easy to get along with. And they needed the patience and diligence of a monk, but also to be able and willing to fight in an instant. Taylor Ray was all these things, and it was moments like this that reminded him of why he loved the job so much.

What he didn't love quite so much was the prospect of a head-on collision with a planet at two hundred thousand kilometers per hour, and he was glad when his frequently over-zealous pilot finally began to decelerate and veer the ship away from the globe's center of mass. Casey had kept the controls on manual, as she preferred to do as much as possible, but as they got closer to the murky brown sphere, it became apparent to all of them that it was no longer capable of supporting life, whether Hedalt, human or anything in between.

"Looks like another dead rock to me, Cap," said Blake, and were it not for the, 'I told you so' swagger to the way he delivered the words, Taylor might have believed he sounded almost disappointed.

"Thank you for your astute observations, Blake," Taylor replied, though the heavy sarcasm was not appreciated by his gruff TacSpec crew member, and he scowled back moodily.

Casey swept into orbit and Taylor switched the viewport to a magnified view of the planet's surface, revealing scorched desert plains, rocky mountains and evidence of rivers and seas that looked to have dried up countless thousands of years earlier.

"There's still a thin atmosphere and the surface gravity is similar to the Hedalt home world, but this would be a harsh environment, even for them," said Satomi, studying the new data. "Both the planet and its moons show evidence of significant volcanic activity in the past, but the planet's core has cooled and there's only a weak magnetosphere."

"So, what you're sayin' is that there's no-one home, right?" said Blake, still smarting from Taylor's sarcastic remark, and retorting with one of his own.

"Oh, there's still some microbial life; I'd say it's probably on a par with your level of intelligence..."

"Oh, burn!" Casey called out, joyfully, while Satomi was still mid-sentence.

"...but, no, I think the chances of finding any Hedalt alive down there are pretty much nil."

"Damn it," said Taylor, clenching a fist. Despite knowing the chances of a contact were slim, he had still let the anticipation build inside him. It was like gambling; the thrill of placing the bet followed by an unbearable suspense and excitement as he waited to see if his numbers turned up, despite knowing the odds were miniscule. After more than thirty jumps, he knew he should have learned to manage his disappointment better, but he couldn't help it; each ghost contact was just as crushingly disappointing as the last.

"So where is the signal coming from then?"

asked Taylor, a little testily.

"That's the really interesting part," Satomi continued, recognizing the dark cloud that was growing above Taylor's head and moving fast to blow it away, before it built to a storm. "The signal isn't actually coming from the planet, but from the second of the three moons." Satomi punched in a sequence of commands and an image of the second moon appeared on the viewport.

The moon was just as dusty-brown and barren-looking as the planet, which didn't fill Taylor with confidence. He pushed himself out of his chair and took a couple of paces towards the screen to get a clearer view, but the moon looked distinctly unremarkable.

"The signal is undeniably Hedalt in origin; if anything, I'd say it was an old comms relay."

"Bah, it's just another damn ghost..." Blake chimed in, sounding as depressed as Taylor looked.

"Perhaps, but let's check it out and confirm," said Taylor, who despite feeling dejected still wanted to present an air of optimism to the crew. Also, the discovery of the signal's origin as coming from the moon did at least mean he got a second throw of the dice. "We could still get lucky. Besides, I'm sure our ace pilot would enjoy an opportunity to skim the surface of that moon, am I right, Casey?"

Casey beamed back at him. "Yes sir, Captain!"

Taylor smiled back; Casey's enthusiasm was infectious, and much-needed. "Okay, take us in and then let's wrap this up so we can all go home."

Casey swung back around, switched the main viewport to the ahead view, and then pulled out of orbit, powering up the ship's massive ion drive engines to maximum as she leveled the nose of the cruiser at the planet's second moon.

Satomi finished her latest piece of analysis and then joined Taylor, standing close by his side, hands pressed behind her back.

"Do you think 'skim the surface' was really the most sensible choice of words?"

Taylor snorted. "It's just a figure of speech, she knows I don't mean for her to literally skim the surface of the moon."

Satomi shook her head. "Really? Like that time when you said, 'Find us a nice spot to land' on the planet four jumps back. The one where she literally landed us on top of a mountain, with about two meters of rock either side of the landing struts stopping us from sliding nine kilometers to our deaths?"

Taylor chewed the inside of his mouth while recalling the landing in question, and then glanced at Satomi, lips curled into a smirk, "But it was one hell of a nice spot to land."

Satomi rolled her eyes, but returned the smile,

and then stared out through the viewport. "At the rate she's going, we'll not so much skim the surface as become a permanent fixture on it."

Taylor scowled at the image of the moon on the viewport, which was growing larger by the second, and Casey was showing no signs of slowing down. "I think I'll take a seat."

Satomi stroked his arm and smiled again. "I don't think taking a seat will help when we hit the moon at zero point two C, but whatever makes you feel better, Captain." Then she turned and was headed back to her station before Taylor had a chance to counter her acerbic remark with a witty and clever one of his own.

Taylor scooted back to his chair, where he remained firmly planted for the remainder of the journey to the moon, nervously tapping on the chair arm as the mass of rock began to dominate the viewport. The speed with which Casey was making the approach had not gone unnoticed by Blake either, who frequently glanced back at Taylor with anxious eyes, looking for his Captain's reassurances that all was well.

"Dontcha think we're coming in a little hot?" queried Blake, finally unable to hold his silence.

"It makes a nice change to have to something to aim for, other than empty space, don't you think?" replied Casey, coolly, though her attention remained sharply focused on the ship's controls.

"I'd be a lot happier if you were aimin' a little off to the side..." added Blake.

Casey laughed. "Just relax, Blakey, and enjoy the ride... Starting deceleration in three... two... one..."

Casey's normally buoyant expression, with cheeks raised high and lips pressed into a near persistent smile, become suddenly more taught and sober as the Nimrod-class cruiser decelerated and veered away from the central axis of the moon. Her hands and feet worked furiously to adjust settings and controls, but never at any point did she look flustered, and as the horizon of the moon filled the viewport and the ship reached a more manageable velocity, she grasped the manual control column and the smile suddenly returned to her eyes.

"We're flying in the atmosphere, what little of it there is; altitude 15,000 and falling..."

Taylor checked the console screen that was built into the arm of his chair. It indicated that the source of the signal was just over four hundred kilometers ahead, but Casey was still moving rapidly. He glanced over to Satomi, who appeared wholly unperturbed by their rapid rate of descent, but Taylor could not maintain his composure any longer and buckled. "Skim the surface was a turn of phrase, Casey, let's cool off a little, please."

"Aw, Captain..."

"That's an order, Casey," said Taylor firmly, "before I lose my lunch."

"Aye, aye, Captain Taylor Ray," Casey replied, though she spoke the words more in the manner of a stroppy teenager who had just been grounded than an officer obeying her Captain.

Casey dialed back the controls and the ship decelerated rapidly and began cruising towards the source of the signal at a leisurely (for Casey) one thousand kilometers per hour at an altitude of five hundred meters. For a ship the size of the Nimrod-class this would have scared the living daylights out of most other crews, but after four years with Casey Valera at the helm, they had all readjusted their definition of 'fast'.

"The source is just ahead, in that enormous region of volcanic rock," said Satomi, pointing unhelpfully at the viewport.

"Got it... swinging around now," said Casey, banking the ship hard left and dropping to two hundred meters. "There it is, dead ahead."

Taylor stood up and stepped closer to the viewport, joined a few moments later by Satomi. Casey slowed the hulking ship to a crawl and began to circle around the object, keeping the nose pointed towards it, more for something to do than out of necessity, since the viewport could focus on the object irrespective of the angle or orientation of the ship.

"Where? All I see is a bunch of rocks..." said Blake, squinting at the viewport as if that would help his 20-20 eyes to see better.

"It's hidden inside that 'bunch of rocks', as you call it" said Satomi, and then she tapped a few commands into her console and the outline of a tall object became visible. From the straight lines and perfect angles, it was clearly artificial in nature.

"I don't get it; why the hell hide a random comms tower in the middle of nowhere?" said Blake, scratching the back of his head and scowling at the screen. "How'd it get there?"

"Unknown, but I'm not detecting any other structures nearby, just the tower," said Satomi.

"Maybe the rest of whatever was here got gobbled up by the lava?" suggested Casey, "This lone tower could be all that's left; sort of like a headstone."

Blake scowled at Casey, "That's a bit dark."

Casey took her hands off the controls and waggled her fingers at Blake, while making a 'wooo' sound like a ghost.

Satomi rolled her eyes, and then moved across to Taylor's command chair. Without asking permission, she punched a sequence of commands into the console in the arm of his chair, and then stood back and looked up at the viewport. A second later, an enhanced image of the comms tower appeared on the viewport.

"If you look closely, the tower has clearly been built on the surface of the pre-existing igneous rock," said Satomi, again pointing at the screen. "If the lava had flowed after the tower's installation, the base of the tower would have been enveloped and covered over."

Taylor rubbed his face, feeling the stubble that he hadn't had a chance to shave off after his rude awaking earlier that morning. He tried to rationalize what he was seeing, but it made no sense. What was a Hedalt comms tower doing on a moon with no other signs of Hedalt military bases or colonies? And a comms tower on its own was useless without at least some supporting structures, and there was also no evidence of a covert listening station. There was just a tower, hidden inside – as Blake had crudely but accurately described – 'a bunch of rocks'.

"Hell, maybe they only got as far as buildin' the tower before Earth Fleet showed up and chased 'em away?" suggested Blake.

"Good theory," said Satomi, grateful for a least one sensible suggestion from Blake, "but Earth Fleet records show we're the first vessel to enter this system."

"Maybe they just abandoned it anyway," Blake continued, "They knew the war was lost so they just high-tailed it outta here."

Satomi shrugged, "It's certainly possible."

"Are we at least able to decipher the signal?" asked Taylor, beginning to feel frustrated again.

Satomi shook her head. "It's essentially just static, as if it was turned on by accident without an actual signal to transmit."

Satomi's last statement triggered a lightbulb moment for Taylor. As the signal hadn't been picked up in the CoreNet previously, why were they able to detect it now? Taylor cocked his head towards Satomi, "Is there a chance this tower could have been turned on recently?"

Satomi's eyes widened as she considered the ramifications of Taylor's question, "Again, it's possible," she said, with matching intrigue. "It would explain why no-one has detected it before now. But, all we know for sure is that it's definitely Hedalt in origin, based on the signal technology and encoding format."

A panel on the mission ops console bleeped and Satomi jogged back to her station to check it. All eyes were on her.

"This is interesting," said Satomi, studying the screen. "I'm detecting an opening two hundred meters north of the comms tower; it appears to be the mouth of a cave."

"I don't see what's particularly interesting about a cave?" said Taylor, letting his frustrations vent out.

Satomi scowled back at him and then folded

her arms tightly across her chest. "It's not the cave that's interesting, Captain," she answered, stressing the word 'Captain' a little too aggressively, "it's what it leads to that is. I think it may be a lava tube."

Taylor's eyebrows raised and eyes widened, as did Casey's, but Blake had the opposite reaction, scrunching his face into a frown.

"Now, that is interesting," said Taylor, sounding like a police inspector that had just uncovered an fascinating new clue. "Casey, can you take us over there to get a closer look? Slowly, please..."

"Aye, aye, Captain Taylor Ray," sang Casey, "It would be my pleasure!"

Blake looked at Casey and then at Satomi and finally at Taylor, noting that all of them appeared to be in on a secret that only he didn't know about. He waited for one of them to explain it to him, but it quickly became apparent that this wasn't about to happen. Eventually, he couldn't stand it any longer and threw his hands up in the air like an annoyed toddler.

"What the hell is a lava tube?!"

FIVE

Casey Valera approached the mouth of the cave with uncharacteristic restraint, as if she was fearful that a dragon might be lurking inside, waiting to swoop out and engulf them in its fiery breath. Everyone on the bridge felt similarly on edge, especially Taylor, who was unable to shake the feeling there was something different and perhaps even dangerous about this moon, compared to the dozens of others they'd investigated over the course of the last four years.

"Satomi, can you direct scans inside the mouth of the cave?" asked Taylor, keeping his eyes fixed on the shadowy opening, which appeared as impenetrable as a black hole. He was curious to know if there was anything beyond the mysterious opening, but also cautious of getting too close. Though it wasn't dragons that he was fearful of, but Hedalt.

Satomi was already busily working at her various consoles, trying to build a picture of what – if anything – was beyond the veil of darkness. There was a brief delay and then she answered, "Not from here, no. For some reason, I can't get a solid scan of anything much below the surface. All I know is that the tunnel beyond the mouth of the cave is deep, though again, I can't get a specific reading. If you took us closer, I might have a better chance."

Taylor sighed, grudgingly accepting the need to be a little more bold. "Okay, understood," he replied, and then he looked over to Casey, who was already peering back at him with one eyebrow raised. "Take us in a little closer, Casey."

"Aye, aye, Captain Taylor Ray," replied Casey, a little more uncertainly than usual. Then she lightly pulsed the thrusters and teased the ship further towards the mouth of the cave, all the while retaining a ready grip on the controls.

"I think I'm getting something now," said Satomi, her intonation rising a little due to her heightened anticipation. "It seems to be a power signature, but it's faint and highly localized..." Then she hesitated, "That's odd..."

"What's odd?" Taylor asked, shifting to the

edge of his seat and twisting to face Satomi. Her face was scrunched into a frown.

"The signature is moving..." Then, eyes wide with fear, her head jolted towards Taylor and she shouted, "Sentry drones!"

Taylor's hand tightened around the arms of his chair and he jerked back to face the viewport, as two Hedalt sentry drones emerged from the darkness. "Take evasive action, go, go, go!" he yelled.

Casey responded instantly, shunting power into the thrusters and wrenching them away from the cave mouth. The ship soared higher into the moon's thin atmosphere, but despite her quick action, the thud of plasma shards slamming into the hull reverberated around the bridge.

"Direct hit... minor damage!" Satomi called out, "Comm systems down... jump engine offline... there's damage to a few other non-critical systems, but it's okay, we're okay!"

"Blake, you're up," Taylor called out, jabbing a finger towards the tactical station, "Take them down, I don't care how!"

"You gottit, Cap," Blake answered with a steely coolness. He worked fast, attempting to get a target lock on the drones with the turrets mounted around the ship's hull, as Casey continued to weave a chaotic course to avoid them. He called over to the pilot's station, "Casey, see if you can get them into the rear firing arc!"

"Sure, but..." Casey began, and it was the 'but' that immediately set Taylor's heart racing.

"But what, Casey?" Taylor cut in, "I need good news, not buts!"

"That's what the but is, Cap," said Casey, whose handling of the controls seemed oddly laid-back, considering they were under attack. "The drones are really struggling to keep up. They should be twice as agile as a ship this size, but I'm giving them the run around easily. It's like there's something wrong with them."

The viewport tracked the drones as another two flashes of plasma raced towards the ship, but Casey evaded them easily.

"What's wrong is that they're not destroyed yet!" Taylor answered, so far forward on his seat that he risked sliding off completely. Just then he heard the reverberant thrum of the ship's turrets unleashing two volleys of rounds, and seconds later both drones exploded.

"That was almost too easy," said Blake, swiveling to face Taylor, "I ain't complainin', don't get me wrong, but Casey's right; those drones should've been a lot faster."

Taylor frowned and massaged his stubbled chin, before turning to Satomi, "Any other activity from the cave mouth?"

Satomi shook her head, "No, nothing more.

But just to add some facts to back up Casey and Blake's instincts, scans of the drones suggested they were operating on minimal power, like their cores had deteriorated, or their cells degraded."

"What does that mean?" asked Taylor.

"If I had to speculate, I'd say it means they were very old," said Satomi, "which means where they came from could have been here for some time. Perhaps even pre-dating the Earth-Hedalt war."

"So it *is* just another damn ghost then," said Blake, sounding more relieved than disappointed.

Satomi shrugged, "Maybe, but even if it is, it's still something we've never come across before," she replied, but Taylor had already seen the sparkle in her eyes; the look that meant the typically prudent Technical Specialist was about to suggest something radical. "I suppose there's really only one way to know for sure..."

Blake shook his head and wagged a finger at her, "Oh no, you can't be serious!"

Satomi smiled back, "Why not? It's what we're out here to do, after all? Besides, our communications systems are down and the jump engines will need at least a couple of hours for repairs, so we've got nothing better to do."

Casey was grinning like a Cheshire cat, finally cottoning on to what Satomi was suggesting, but Taylor had known from the moment she had uttered the word, 'maybe'. He nodded at Satomi and then turned to Casey. "Looks like we're in for a spot of cave diving... Assuming you think you're up to it, Casey?"

"Aye, aye, Captain Taylor Ray!" beamed Casey with uncontained excitement, before she turned back the controls, practically fizzing with enthusiasm. But Casey's gleeful murmurs were drowned out by the resonant slap of Blake clapping his hand over his eyes, and dragging it down his across his face. He didn't feel excited. He felt like a man who'd just bet all his money on red, and lost.

SIX

Casey spun the ship around and dropped down into a hover directly in front of the cave. It was a single, seamless maneuver that was skillful, elegant and flamboyantly unnecessary. This time, however, Blake made sure that the forward cannons and turrets were trained squarely on the opening, just in case there were any more unexpected arrivals.

"It's definitely a lava tube," said Satomi, focusing additional scans into the mouth of the cave. Then, for the benefit of soothing Blake's already aggravated mood – he looked like he was ready to punch something or someone – she elucidated. "A lava tube is basically a cave that forms when a lava flow hardens on the surface, but then continues to flow underneath. Once the subsurface lava flow has drained, a cave or lava tube is left behind; sometimes a pretty big one."

Blake thought for a moment and then his eyes widened and his mouth fell open in a proverbial light-bulb moment. "Wow, hold on a second... so you're thinkin' it could be a cave that's big enough to hide an outpost?"

"Yes, but not just an outpost; depending on the size of the lava tube, it's possible that one could contain a base the size of a city," added Taylor, feeding on the aura of excitement that now filled the bridge. "A base that's neatly hidden from view and from our scans."

"Speaking of scans," Satomi cut back in, "I now understand why we can't penetrate the surface. There's something about the composition of the igneous rock that is essentially acting as a shield against all sensors. So while I don't know how large this lava tube is, I've scanned the cave mouth and it is wide enough."

Casey let out a sound that seemed to be part laugh, part squeal.

"C'mon guys!" said Blake, suddenly remembering why they were hovering in front of the cave entrance in the first place. "You're not seriously considerin' taking the ship inside?"

"Why not?" said Taylor, shrugging.

Blake almost choked. "Why not? Apart from

the obvious craziness of flying into a damn cave, there could be a whole squadron of Hedalt Corvettes in there, that's why not!"

"I don't think so," said Taylor, calmly. "That comms tower is just putting out static, which suggests it's a malfunction. And those drones were relics too; just an automated response to unwanted guests. Besides, if there were really a squadron of Corvettes on the other side of that cave mouth, I'd imagine that we'd have plasma shards flying at us by now."

"That's a whole lotta assumptions, Cap," said Blake, folding his arms, but then he seemed to have an epiphany and his expression softened. "But, seein' as we're here then what the hell. There could be some good salvage bounty in it, I guess."

"Always the mercenary, hey Blakey?" said Casey, winking at him.

"I'm the only one here who has their head screwed on straight!" replied Blake, huffily, swinging his chair to face the tactical console again. "Unless you've all forgotten, I'm only out here for the money, not the company."

Casey pouted at him, playfully, "I'll try not to take that personally..."

"Don't try too hard..." replied Blake with a mischievous grin, and then he cocked his head back towards Taylor and said, "I assume you'll want me to keep the weapons armed, Cap?" He left a pause for effect and added, "Or, are ya so sure there ain't an army of belligerent aliens through that hole that you're happy for us to fly in with our pants down?"

"What a charming image..." Casey chirped in, without looking at Blake.

"I'm sure you're going to keep them powered up no matter what I say," Taylor replied, dryly. "So yes, Tactical Specialist Meade, please keep your itchy finger on the trigger."

Blake didn't answer and just returned his attention to the tactical console, checking rows of indicators in turn. "Forward cannons, ready; dorsal turrets, ready; ventral turrets, ready, aft turrets, ready. All weapon systems armed an' ready to blow up whatever nasty alien bastard is in that cave, sir."

"Thank you, Blake," said Taylor, patiently.

Other Captains would have reprimanded Blake for being such a mouthy pain-in-the-ass, but over the last four years, Taylor had come to understand that Blake's bravado was really a mask for nerves and anxiety – a coping mechanism of sorts – so he cut him the slack he needed. When it came down to it, Blake was a proficient TacSpec officer; one who wouldn't buckle under pressure. Besides, Taylor knew that no-one on the ship was without their flaws and little idiosyncrasies. Regular people placed under the same conditions would have torn each other limb-from-limb after only a few months together, but the tiny percentage of Earth Fleet crew who passed for DSR missions had a forbearance and patience that that made them uniquely qualified for the job.

"Alright, Casey, take us in," said Taylor, and then added, with considerably greater emphasis, "SLOWLY..."

"Aye, aye, Captain Taylor Ray," Casey chirruped, without even the slightest hint of disappointment about the order to go slow. She was aware of only one other pilot that had ever attempted to navigate a lava tube, and that had been in an Emissary-class scout, half the size of the mightier Nimrod. Not only that, but the pilot had also scraped the hull against the cave wall during transit through the entrance tunnel, forcing them to abort mid-mission due to the structural damage it had caused to the ship and cave. Casey was not going to ruin the opportunity to write her name into the annals of Earth Fleet pilot history by hot-rodding into the cave mouth and botching her attempt in the same way.

Keeping the controls on manual, and maintaining a laser-like focus, Casey drew her pilot's viewport closer and focused her gaze inside. This gave her a panoramic view outside the ship that updated in real-time as she moved her head. It was designed for use in combat operations, but was also ideal for navigating through tight spaces, like the cave mouth. She activated the forward flood lights and engaged the thrusters, edging through the opening. Taylor kept a close watch on the distance readings from the console in his chair, though he never doubted for a second that Casey could pull this maneuver off. Casey Valera was the most gifted, natural pilot he'd ever seen, as well as the kookiest. He glanced over to Satomi, who appeared calm and focused, as she always did, and then at Blake, who was coiled tighter than a cobra and looked like he'd been holding his breath for the last few minutes.

"Damn it, Blake, breathe out before you burst," Taylor called out, which would have normally drawn a mirthful titter from Casey, but there was no reaction at all. She had already zoned everything else out, as if she and the ship were now one. Unseen to Taylor, however, Satomi glanced over at her Captain and smiled.

The tunnel suddenly narrowed, causing the collision alerts to sound and Blake's blood pressure to rise higher, but Casey remained levelheaded, adjusting the controls with a lightness of touch that a surgeon would have envied, and the angry alarms ceased. Blake exhaled, audibly, and a moment later the Nimrod-class cruiser exited the tunnel and emerged into the lava tube. Casey let out a long, low whistle as her navigational sensors revealed the scale of the internal structure. It was truly cavernous.

Taylor punched up all the exterior flood-lights, but the beams barely made a difference to the veil of darkness inside; it was like being in deep space, but without the comforting companionship of starlight.

"It's reading as eight point two kilometers across at the widest point," said Satomi, absorbed by the data appearing on her screen, "and I'm detecting metals and structures on the surface, towards the boundaries; definitely not natural."

Taylor glanced over at Blake and their eyes met with instant understanding between them. Taylor nodded and Blake returned his attention to his console, with all traces of his former flippancy gone. When the circumstances dictated it, Blake's senses would suddenly be primed, like drawing a sharpened blade from a dusty scabbard.

"Are you detecting any vessels or energy signatures?" asked Taylor, feeling his pulse start to quicken. There was a pause before Satomi replied, which felt like a lifetime.

"No ships, at least none on the surface or that have active power cores, but the structures are certainly large enough to be hangars that could contain dozens of Corvettes," Satomi finally answered. "I am detecting a faint power signature; possibly the source of whatever is powering the comms tower outside."

Taylor rubbed his stubbled chin and considered his next action. It was clear they had discovered a hidden Hedalt installation, and though the weak power source and encounter with the archaic drones outside still suggested it was a ghost – the nickname that Earth Fleet personnel gave to installations that were long-deserted – he didn't want to take any chances.

"Take us closer to the power source, Casey," said Taylor. "But stay alert; we may need to get out of here in a hurry in case any more of those drones show up. Or worse..."

Casey adjusted course and increased power to the thrusters, while nervously muttering, "Aye, aye, Captain Taylor Ray," under her breath.

Taylor enabled the image intensifier and focused in on the target location. The viewport switched modes and a few seconds later an ethereal image of a vast complex of structures materialized on the screen. He checked the display on his chair's console screen, which was showing a wireframe representation of the surface layout that had been constructed from Satomi's sensor scans.

"From the design, I'd say it's definitely a starship base, and definitely Hedalt in origin," commented Taylor. "No way of telling how long it's been here, though."

"I don't see any ships on the landin' pads," Blake added, "but Satomi's right; a lotta those structures sure look like hangars, and I'm pickin' up some sorta sub-structure too."

"What kind of sub-structure?" asked Taylor, checking his panel to assess the readings.

"I ain't gotta clue, but whatever's underneath all this, there's a helluva lot of it. There's maybe double the area of the surface structures hidden down there."

Casey interrupted to give a status report, "We're three hundred meters from the source, altitude five hundred."

"Okay, keep it stead..."

"Power readings are spiking!" Satomi cut across them both; her voice urgent, almost frantic.

Taylor pushed himself out of the chair. "Where? Focus the viewport on the source."

Satomi rapidly input the commands and the image on the viewport switched to show a thick, rectangular tower with a spherical top half, which was spinning towards them.

"It's a watch tower!" shouted Blake.

Taylor ran forward and grabbed the back of the pilot's chair, "Casey, get us out of range of that tower, smartly!"

Casey didn't answer with her customary response and instead instantly sprang into action, yanking back hard on the controls and pushing the thruster lever forwards. The ship responded, fighting against the moon's gravity, and began accelerating hard, surging away from the Hedalt base and climbing rapidly. But then another alarm sounded on the bridge and the Nimrod-class cruiser was rocked, as if the hull had been pummeled with a giant baseball bat.

"We're hit!" shouted Satomi.

"No shit!" Blake called out in reply, but then held his tongue as Taylor stumbled from Casey's chair to the back of Blake's and glowered down at him.

"Just take out that watch tower, now!" shouted Taylor, struggling to stay on his feet as the ship lurched and buffeted from side-to-side.

Blake uncoiled and sprang into action, targeting the watch tower with the aft turret and opening fire in a matter of seconds. The main viewport showed the rounds raking across the spherical upper portion of the tower, and a second later it exploded.

"Good shot, Blake!" cried Taylor, but his elation was short-lived.

"I'm losing altitude!" shouted Casey.

"Satomi, damage report!"

"Minor hull breach," Satomi called out, before another violent shimmy almost threw her from her chair. "The ablative armor took the brunt of the hit, but we've got red lights across a dozen secondary systems and..."

"Just tell us why we're falling..." Taylor shouted, cutting Satomi off mid-sentence.

There was a brief pause, while Satomi scanned ahead on the damage report, "Four ventral thrusters have been destroyed."

"Can we still make it out of this cave?"

The question was directed at Satomi, but it was Casey that responded. "No way, Cap, we don't have enough thrust to make the climb," she said, wrestling with the controls, "and even if I boosted us up there with the main engines, she's writhing around like a python; chances are we'd just end up smashed against the cave wall."

"Damn it!" Taylor cursed, gripping the back of Blake's chair even more tightly. If they couldn't get out there was only one option left, but he knew the crew wouldn't like it. He didn't like it himself.

"Casey, you're going to have to set us down on one of the landing pads on the base below."

"What, are you crazy?!" Blake shouted, craning his neck to stare up a Taylor. "If they're firin' at us then this ain't no ghost base!"

"We don't have a choice," Taylor hit back. Then he jabbed a finger towards Blake, as if he was pointing a gun, "I want you to keep the cannons trained on the surface and take out anything that even looks like it's moving, got it?" Blake didn't answer and just gritted his teeth. "Then as soon as we land, prepare the expedition gear. We'll have to inspect the damage and make repairs on the ground." Blake looked ready to argue back, but Taylor didn't allow it. "Is that clear, Specialist Meade?"

Blake pressed his teeth evenly more tightly together and spun his chair back to face his console. "Yes, sir," he growled.

Taylor staggered back behind Casey's chair and rested his hand on her shoulder. He added gentle pressure, causing her to look away from her pilot's viewport and into his eyes.

"Casey, if anyone can land this thing it's you. Can you handle it?"

Casey's eyes wavered; she looked terrified, like a kid on their first day of school, but she managed to nod her head in short staccato movements and say, "Aye, aye, Captain Taylor Ray," though the words lacked any of her usual brightness and confidence.

The ship was shaken again as Taylor lurched back to his command chair and practically fell into it. Casey angled the nose of the ship back down towards the Hedalt base, battling with the controls, which were fighting against her like a toddler having a tantrum due to the damaged reaction control system thruster array.

"Energy surge ahead... it's another watch tower!" Satomi shouted, but this time Blake needed no warning, firing the forward cannons and reducing the tower to rubble, before the spherical turret had chance to engage them.

"Well done, Blake!" Taylor cried out, and though he couldn't see it, the corner of Blake's mouth twisted into a satisfied smile.

Suddenly, the ship veered violently off course, forcing Casey to make a series of rapid adjustments; her hands and feet moving so fast they were almost a blur. Taylor observed her in amazement, thankful for his kooky, purple sneaker-wearing pilot more than ever, knowing that ninety-nine percent of the other DSR pilots in Earth Fleet would have likely already crashed by this point.

"We've lost another RCS thruster!" Casey called out, reaching forward and adjusting the power distribution of the remaining thrusters to compensate for the loss.

"Just keep going, we're almost there!" Taylor called out, aware that the landing pad was approaching fast; faster than he would like. He glanced down to check the console in the arm of his chair, reading out the distances in his head.

Two hundred meters...

One hundred meters...

Fifty meters...

Come on Casey, slow this hulk of metal down!

Casey's concentration had become almost

transcendental, so much so that she had become deaf to the clamor on the bridge; her world had become only what she could see through her pilot's viewport. Twenty meters from the deck she shunted all power into the remaining ventral thrusters and pushed them beyond their red line, cutting the ship's descent velocity to a crawl with only five meters to spare. She kicked out the landing struts, levelled off the ship and dropped it onto the deck as delicately as if it had been a routine landing on automatic. Pushing her viewport away from her eyes, she flipped a sequence of switches to power down the main reactor and RCS system, which was on the brink of blowing up, and then slumped back into her chair, letting every muscle in her body go slack.

"Landing complete, Cap," she said, after blowing out a sigh.

Taylor slammed his hands down on the arms of his chair, "Incredible, as always, Casey!" he cried, with the jubilant relief of someone who had just played Russian Roulette and won. He wasn't just blowing smoke, either – the deftness of the landing under such challenging and stressful circumstances was a simply amazing feat of starship piloting. Casey tipped the seat back, slanted her head towards Taylor and returned a relieved, but also roguish smile that was much more like the Casey that Taylor knew so well.

Taylor twisted to face the missions ops station, "Satomi, are there any other signs of movement on the base? Ships powering up, ground soldiers, drones, anything?"

Satomi shook her head, "Negative, Captain. The rest of base is still completely dead, apart from the same weak power signature we detected initially." She continued to cycle through her scan readings and then looked up at Taylor, "The watch towers were just automated defense systems, and like the drones they were badly decayed. The plasma shard that hit us wasn't at full power, which is lucky, because if it had been we'd already be atoms."

"You call bein' crippled inside this lava thing *luck*?" Blake chimed in. His tone was more sour than a lemon.

"Any enemy contact where we all walk away is a good one, Blake," Taylor answered, "Now, cut the attitude so we can figure out how to repair the ship and can get off this rock."

Rather than glower back at Taylor, Blake actually looked embarrassed, "Sorry, Cap. I know I speak out of turn sometimes. I don't mean nothin' by it."

"Sometimes..." murmured Satomi, but not loud enough that Blake could hear.

"It's okay Blake, I know it was a close call. But right now we need you focused. Break out the expedition gear, but make sure every turret on this ship stays hot. We're not out of danger yet."

Blake nodded and then punched a sequence of controls on his console to set the turrets to perimeter defense mode. He then sprang out of his seat and was half-way to the door leading off the bridge when Satomi suddenly spoke up.

"Captain..."

Taylor knew instantly that the fact she was calling him 'Captain' and not 'Taylor' didn't bode well. "What's up Satomi? And please don't tell me it's more bad news."

"Well, I suppose it's more what you'd call unusual news than bad news. Though it's also not good news," Satomi replied, sounding as uncertain as her description had been unclear.

"Spit it out already..." snapped Blake, impatiently; he'd stopped on the door threshold, waiting to hear what Satomi had to say.

"We've lost our uplink to the CoreNet."

Taylor stood and hurried over to the mission ops station, "What, completely lost connection? I didn't think that was possible."

"It shouldn't be," said Satomi. "Given how the system was designed and the nature of super-luminal signal transmission, we should always be linked to the CoreNet, through the Fabric, even at this range." Satomi worked the console, checking their position relative to their previous location.

"We're unusually distant from the nearest super-luminal transceiver, but while the signal may take longer, we should still always have a link. Except down here, it's completely cut off."

"What does that mean?" asked Blake, still hovering by the door. "Is that bad?"

Taylor sighed. "The only reason a ship would ever lose its connection to the CoreNet is if it had been destroyed. Basically, Earth Fleet is going to assume that we're dead."

"But, that's good isn't it?" Casey chimed in. "We'll get sent a rescue?"

"We're out in frontier territory here, Casey," said Taylor, shaking his head, "it could be months before Earth Fleet considers a search and rescue mission, if they even bother to send one at all. As harsh as it sounds, the cost and risk of sending a SAR mission out this far, just for a four-person deep-space recon expedition, is probably too high. They could end up losing two crews, and two ships."

"What? That's... cold," said Casey, and she shuddered as if an icy breeze had just whipped past her.

"So, whadda we do, Cap?" added Blake, surprisingly calmly, but also with a resigned air. Taylor had half-expected Blake to blow up at the news that a rescue mission was unlikely, but then he realized Blake would already know the guidelines for SAR operations, since they fell under the remit of the TacSpec division. If they were to get out of the lava tube, they'd have to do it without outside help. Blake knew that, which is why he'd switched modes.

"We stick to the plan," said Taylor, assertively. "We fix up the ship and then haul ass home, before Earth Fleet decides to write our obituaries and sell off all our assets."

Blake's eyes widened, but he, like the others, knew that Taylor wasn't joking.

SEVEN

Taylor, Satomi and Casey were gathered in the rear cargo bay when Blake bustled in, laden with four sets of expedition gear, each set consisting of body armor, a powerful sidearm with solid slug and explosive round clips, stored in pouches on the armored vest, and a backpack with various tools and medical supplies. His face and body were barely discernable underneath the mass of equipment.

"You didn't have to bring it all at once, you know?" laughed Casey, "You look like a walking storeroom."

Blake staggered further into the cargo bay and then unceremoniously dumped all the kit on the deck. He sucked in a breath and let it out, resting his aching hands on his hips, "You're welcome, Casey."

Taylor picked up the body armor and then glanced over to the environment suits hanging up on the wall, "We're going to have to put the environment suits on over this armor," he said slipping his on.

"That'll be a tight fit," grumbled Blake.

"Maybe for you," said Casey, "Perhaps you should cut down on the midnight snacks?"

Blake beat his chest like a gorilla, "This is pure muscle, Casey. I'm not surprised you don't know what that looks like..."

"Alright, knock it off you two," said Taylor, picking up a second set of body armor and slinging it towards Blake, who caught it. "Let's suit up quickly; I don't want to spend any more time here than necessary."

Blake had been right, though; the armor was a tight fit underneath the environment suits, but the suit was required in order to venture outside, into the moon's thin, toxic atmosphere. There was another reason too; if it turned out they didn't have the parts needed to repair the ship, they'd have to hunt for them in the mysterious structures hidden inside the lava tube. And to get to the buildings they'd have to traverse the distance on foot. If there were any Hedalt still alive on the base, they hadn't granted them the courtesy of extending a docking tunnel to their ship.

Taylor finished donning his environment suit and powered it up, checking the status display in the visor, which showed his vital signs and information about the environment outside the suit; currently just the normal atmosphere inside the ship. A few seconds later a red chevron appeared in the top-right of his display, followed by searing red text in the middle of his visor, which read, 'CoreNet connection lost. Abort mission. Immediately re-establish connection to CoreNet.' Taylor angrily dismissed the alert with a flick of his eyes. *That's what I'm trying to do...*

He waited until the names of the other three crew members flashed up in his visor display, indicating that their suits were online too, and then stepped in front of the bay door.

"Okay, Satomi, depressurize the bay and extend the ramp," Taylor ordered, while removing the sidearm from its magnetic stow on the hip of his environment suit. Satomi nodded with some difficulty, due to the restrictive suit, and turned to the control panel. A few seconds later, Taylor could see the atmosphere reading start to change as the breathable air was blown out and replaced by the toxic carbon monoxide based atmosphere inside the lava tube.

Taylor cautiously stepped a few paces down the ramp, but was then passed by Blake, who raced ahead, weapon raised.

"Take it easy, Blake," cautioned Taylor, but Blake waved him off.

"If they were goin' to shoot at us they woulda done it already," said Blake, checking underneath the ship and then quickly surveying the surrounding area, but everything was as deathly quiet as a tomb. "We're clear down here, come on out."

Taylor finished moving out, followed by Satomi and Casey who exited the ship side-by-side; neither had their weapons drawn.

There was no real need for Taylor or Blake to have their weapons drawn either, because the turrets on the Nimrod-class cruiser were still all active and in perimeter defense mode. Even if a full platoon of Hedalt soldiers suddenly charged out of hiding, they would be cut down in an instant by the ship's powerful weapons. However, holding the sidearm made Blake feel more in control, helping to instill within him the courage to take the lead. Taylor welcomed the reassuring feeling of being prepared to defend himself too, but the difference was that Taylor knew it was just a false sense of security, whereas the weapon made Blake feel genuinely indomitable.

They gathered together on the smooth artificial surface of the landing pad, sheltered under the hull of the ship and further protected by the ventral turret directly above their heads, which was ever watchful for signs of enemy contact. The ship's floodlights were the only source of illumination other than the torches in their environment suits, but the light didn't penetrate far and it felt like they'd landed in a void that was even emptier than space.

Casey concentrated the lights in her suit helmet into a focused column and peered up at the hull to inspect the damage, using the image enhancement feature of her helmet visor to zoom in on the worst affected sections of the ship.

"How bad is it, Casey?" asked Taylor after his pilot had been silent for a few moments.

Casey didn't answer right away and instead flitted around under the ship, swinging stylishly around the landing struts as if they were lamp posts, while inspecting the different points of damage. The display in her visor updated in real-time to show the damage report for the specific areas that she focused on.

"It's not all that bad, Cap," Casey eventually answered, while pirouetting around the aft, port-side landing strut to face the others again. She sounded upbeat. "The ablative armor can be patched up with spares we already have on the ship, and the secondary systems are no problem. Mostly, it's a case of replacing fried circuits and repairing broken conduits, and the repair drones can take care of that." She looked over at Satomi and even through the visor Satomi could see she was grinning, "The water heating system is down in section three, though."

"Great," said Satomi. "It would have to be the section where my quarters are."

"I think whether or not you can take a hot shower is fairly low down on the list of priorities, Satomi," said Taylor, sarcastically.

"You might not think so once we finally get out of these environment suits; I feel like even my sweat is sweating."

"Nice image, thanks..." said Taylor, suddenly compelled to picture how sweat might sweat. A bit like when someone says something like, 'don't think of a pink elephant', which then makes it impossible *not* to think of a pink elephant. "Casey, what about the damaged RCS thrusters?" Taylor added, trying to focus his mind away from Satomi's sweating sweat.

Casey had continued to study the damage report while Satomi and Taylor had been bantering. "They're totally shot, I'm afraid, Cap," she said, sounding suddenly deflated, "and we don't have any replacements in the hold; we had to strip those for other components about five jumps back. We're going to have to find compatible replacements, or at least the raw materials or core components so I can fabricate substitutes."

"Damn it," cursed Taylor. He stowed his weapon on his hip again and peered out towards the hulking structures, barely visible in the distance. "Well, we are on what appears to be a starship base, so hopefully it shouldn't be too hard to find what we need."

"Assumin' the place ain't crawlin' with Hedalt soldiers..." Blake chimed in.

"As you said, if that was the case, we'd have known about it by now," said Taylor, quick to rebuff Blake's doom-mongering by throwing his own logic back in his face. Pointing out the worst-case scenario was something that Blake did in particularly stressful or dangerous situations. Perversely, it actually helped him to cope, the logic being that if he was expecting the worst then he could never be caught off guard. Also, if the situation then proved to be anything less than a total, unmitigated disaster, it would seem like a minor victory and make him feel more at ease. It didn't make sense to Taylor, who preferred to deal with the cold, hard facts and stay focused on positives, no matter how dire their situation became, but it worked for Blake and that was fine with him. The only problem was when Blake's excessive negativity overflowed and started to drag down the others, as it was threatening to do now. It was one thing for Blake to spout negativity when they were in the relative safety of a fully-functioning cruiser, but quite another when the danger was real and present. Everyone had to believe that they would make it through, otherwise they were destined to fail.

"As Satomi already suggested, it was probably just a malfunction that triggered power to the comms tower, and those watch tower guns are likely an automated response to an enemy ship."

"Yeah, well I hope you're right," Blake replied, but nothing about the way he answered suggested he believed Taylor's optimism was warranted.

"Hey, hope has nothing to do with it," said Taylor, not letting Blake off the hook. "I know we can do this. Boldness be my friend."

"There he goes, quotin' Dickens again..." said Blake, winking at Casey.

"It's Shakespeare for crying out loud!" yelled Satomi, taking the bait again.

"What it is, is advice," said Taylor, cutting back in. "Advice to all of us. I know this is a bad situation. I know you're afraid – hell, I am too – but we're going to make it through. Captain's orders." He was looking directly at Blake as he said this, but it was actually Casey that answered, with her usual, "Aye, aye, Captain Taylor Ray."

Taylor used the command interface in his suit to concentrate the ship's floodlights towards the closest structure, casting anything outside of the range of the beam into an eerie darkness. The glow just about managed to light their path, but it also highlighted four other landing pads, with what looked like many more extending into the darkness to either side of the beam.

"We're lucky that this place never came online while the war was still ongoing," said Satomi, doing some quick math in her head and estimating there to be twenty landing pads, just in the small section of the base they were in. "There would have been enough ships here to turn the tide against us."

"I wonder why they never got around to using it?" mused Casey, who was awed by the prospect of so many ships in a sort of morbidly curious way.

"Let's keep the speculation to a minimum, and focus on getting our ship repaired," Taylor cut in. "Blake, you're on point, take us to that structure over there, smartly."

Blake moved out in front, holding his weapon at low-ready and stepping swiftly, but also cautiously, minding his footing with each pace forward. Casey highlighted in her visor the damaged systems that could be repaired with resources already available on the ship, and set them in priority order for repair, before initiating the repair drones and following on at the rear of the line. As she stepped out from underneath the belly of the ship, she heard the drones buzzing out of their compartments and setting to work, like an army of spiders repairing the broken strands of their webs.

As the structure of the Hedalt base came closer, the sheer scale of the installation became more apparent to Taylor, and it gave him the creeps. He and his crew had encountered five small ghost installations during their four-year mission, but this was the first one that truly lived up to the name. Taylor felt as though he was walking through a cemetery, but one where the residents could spring up at any moment, like undead warriors, clawing their way out of the dirt in some ancient fantasy movie. He looked up, instinctively expecting to see stars, but there was only blackness; the starlight completely cut out by the vast awning of volcanic rock. Starfields, nebulae and galaxies had taken the place of sunrises, blue skies and green fields as a way for Taylor to feel grounded and connected with the universe, and whenever he felt low, he would go to the observation deck on the ship and just lie back, staring out into the vastness of space. He wasn't claustrophobic – if he had been then he'd never have passed selection for DSR – but if he went for too long without the comforting presence of starlight, he would become irritable and depressed. He tore his eyes away from the expanse of nothing above his head and tried not to think about it, but his gut twisted at the thought of being stuck inside this cave for the rest of his life. Or, far worse, to die inside it, cut off from the universe, and never again see starlight.

As they got closer to the structures and the torches on their environment suits illuminated the exterior walls in a clear, white light, it became more obvious that the place had been deserted for a long time. There was a general air of neglect but, more than that, everything seemed old and worn. Metals were tarnished and a bronze dust coated everything, which Taylor presumed must have been blown in through the tunnel from outside over a period of decades or even centuries. This bothered Taylor; the war had ended only six years previously, and the level of deterioration was too extreme for such a short period of time. It only added to the weight of evidence that the base likely pre-dated their conflict with the Hedalt by some time.

"Somethin' about this place don't sit right," said Blake, as if he'd been reading Taylor's thoughts. "I can't put my finger on it, but I don't like it."

"Just focus on the mission Blake," answered Taylor, again trying to head off Blake's tendency towards overt negativity. "But, for what it's worth, I know how you feel. Let's just get what we need and then we can all head back to Earth."

"There's a door here," said Satomi, who had

gone ahead. "It's a standard Hedalt airlock system, probably an emergency exit. I believe I can feed power to it from my suit and bypass it fairly easily."

Taylor nodded and they all watched as Satomi worked, hacking into the door control system with the proficiency of someone who'd done it a hundred times before. Less than a minute elapsed before the door slid open, dragging back a thick layer of grime as it slid into its housing. Blake swept forward and checked inside, sweeping his weapon from side to side, and then called out, "Clear!" Satomi wasted no time and swiftly moved through and over to the counterpart airlock door that was all that now separated them from the internal structure.

"There's still air pressure on the inside," Satomi called back to the others, her voice a little shakier than normal; this ghost base was starting to seem less ghostly by the minute. Satomi checked her own vital signs in her visor and noted that her pulse was steady at around ninety, almost three times her resting rate, which explained why she felt so wired. Taylor used to joke about Satomi's abnormally low heart-rate, telling her that he always had to hack the medical computer system in order for it to accept her results, because the computer wouldn't allow him to input a heart rate any lower than forty. *It was either hack the system or enter your results under DECEASED* he'd tell her, smirking.

"Is the air breathable?" said Taylor. The news was unexpected and he instinctively placed his hand on his weapon, magnetized to his hip.

Satomi continued to check the readings and then glanced back and returned an anxious nod.

"If there's still air inside then there could still be Hedalt soldiers inside," said Blake, looking intently at Taylor. Unlike his Captain, he had never put his weapon away. "I say we move in hot; ain't no sense in takin' chances."

Taylor nodded, "Boldness be my friend..." he muttered again, as much to himself as Blake.

Blake raised he weapon and tapped the barrel with this index finger, "This is the only friend I need in there."

Taylor then looked to the others, who each stared back at him, nervously awaiting his next command. "You all know the drill. Let's get this done."

EIGHT

With his weapon drawn, Taylor moved alongside Satomi, who had already closed the outer airlock door and was working on circumventing the lock mechanism to the inner door. Casey had moved to the opposite side next to Blake, who immediately noticed that her weapon was still magnetically attached to her environment suit.

"Hey, you're gonna need that, Casey," said Blake, tapping the handgun fixed to her thigh.

"I hate these things," Casey answered, as if she was describing a particularly unpleasant party hors d'oeuvre. "Besides, that's why I moved next to you, Blakey, so that you can protect me."

"I mean it Casey, stop messin' around," Blake

hit back, his voice lacking any of the playfulness that characterized their usual exchanges. "We don't know what's waitin' for us in there, and I've gotta bad feeling 'bout this place."

"Okay, I'm sorry..." said Casey, pulling the handgun away from its magnetic mount and loading it. Her voice betrayed a hint of embarrassed irritation. "You don't have to worry about me, Blake, I can take care of myself."

"I know you can, Casey, I just don't want you..." he paused, and the sudden awkwardness between them was palpable. Taylor and Satomi exchanged knowing glances; both had seen this enough times to know what was happening, and to stay out of it. "I just don't wanna be the only target for any Hedalt freaks that're inside to shoot at," Blake went on, carefully adjusting his sentence to save further embarrassment. "At least if we all go in there with weapons raised, it's only a one in four chance they'll shoot me first."

Casey smiled and look visibly relieved, "Nice idea, Blakey, but we all know that the Hedalt shoot the ugliest humans first, so I'm afraid you're out of luck not matter what happens..."

Blake laughed, "Just stay outta my firin' line, Casey; it'd be a shame if I shot you by..." he paused, but this time for dramatic effect, "*mistake.*"

Taylor waited for their little verbal interchange to run its course. It had been obvious to him and Satomi for the last two years that Casey and Blake genuinely cared about each other, but neither was able to articulate or even admit their feelings, which is why they constantly teased and bantered with each other instead. On the rare occasions when their shields of humor failed, they became awkward, but usually not for long until one of them managed to raise shields again, as Blake had done on this occasion.

Satomi had been ready for the last minute, but like Taylor, she had known to wait. "Okay, I'm opening the door in three... two... one... now!"

The heavy airlock door slid open and Blake rushed inside, checking the angles with polished professionalism, followed by Casey, Taylor and then Satomi in a classic four-person room-clearing action, but there was nothing inside but dust and murky darkness.

"Looks like there's no-one home, after all," said Blake, with a detectable sense of relief, but he still felt exposed and on edge, "not in this section, anyhow."

"The internal environmental systems seem to be set to some kind of extended low-power mode," said Satomi, checking the readings in the room. "There's breathable air, plus Earth-normal gravity and heat, but not much. It's barely more than ten degrees Celsius in here."

"Maybe they didn't have chance to shut

everything down before they left," said Casey who, like Taylor, preferred optimism to pessimism. "Or maybe they expected to return. They could have just evacuated and powered down the base to keep it a secret; after all, we never found it until now."

"It's certainly possible, Casey," admitted Taylor. "They could have evacuated and switched everything to minimal power to hide it from our sensors, but then we won the war and they never got the opportunity to come back."

"Or they could still be in here, waiting for us." offered Blake, unwilling to pass up an opportunity to present a bleaker argument.

Taylor let Blake's glum comment slide, and turned to Satomi. "Close the inner door and then let's see if we can locate a computer that can tell us where to find a workshop, hangar or parts storage bay."

Satomi acknowledged the order, backtracked to the airlock and repeated the procedure to close the inner door. It slid shut with a thud, but then the control panel flashed and a garbled stream of letters and numbers streamed across the display.

"Captain..." she called back, and Taylor rushed to her side.

"What's happening?" asked Taylor, looking at the random gibberish that was flashing past too quickly to read.

"I don't know, it just started when I closed the door." Satomi replied as her pulse shot over one hundred. A few seconds later, they all felt the powerful thud of relays opening somewhere deep beneath them, and then the lights inside the corridor flickered on, bathing them in a harsh white glow that was almost clinical.

"Satomi, what the hell did you do?!" shouted Blake, spinning around like a yo-yo and aiming his weapon at each new shadow that appeared.

"Take it easy Blake," said Taylor, sounding calm, but also feeling his heart rate accelerate faster than a starship, "watch the other entrances, we don't want to get taken by surprise."

Blake rushed ahead, checking through each of the five double doors that had just been revealed thanks to the harsh strip lights overhead; two on either side of the corridor and one at the far end.

"I don't know what happened, Captain, I'm sorry," said Satomi, breathlessly. "Perhaps I tripped some circuits when I closed the airlock door, or it could just be another malfunction, like with the comms tower."

"It's okay, just stay calm," Taylor said again, as much to himself as to the others. "Can you get that door open again?"

Satomi returned her attention to the control panel, but this time she was unable to bypass the system. "Negative, it's jammed up tight; we'll have to find another way out."

Taylor cursed silently. The last thing they needed was to be trapped inside without a known means of escape.

Up ahead, Blake had finished checking the doors and was satisfied that they were still alone.

"We're still clear, Cap," said Blake jogging back to rejoin the group. "There are four rooms leadin' off from this corridor, and the doors are all unlocked. They all look the same to me, full of some strange-looking chambers."

"Let's just take the first door and go one room at a time," said Taylor. "We treat every room like it could be full of Hedalt, got it?"

The group chorused 'yes sir' in a broken harmony of anxious voices and then followed Blake up to the nearest door. Repeating their tightly-choreographed maneuver, they burst inside but again the room was unoccupied. Taylor attached his weapon back in its magnetic stow and examined the new space, while Blake returned to the door to keep watch.

Taylor observed that the room was roughly the size of a large two-bed apartment, like the 'Super Deluxe' apartment overlooking the Columbia river in Astoria that he had been banking his DSR pay in order to buy, when he finally hung up his Captain's hat. He wondered why his mind had suddenly latched on to that particular example, and found himself thinking about Earth and the life he'd planned for himself; a place to set aside the memories of war and the loneliness of DSR missions. He had imagined inviting Satomi there one day, to explore if there was a chance of a future for them outside of Earth Fleet and to see if their relationship could perhaps grow beyond the platonic and professional. But like the apartment, it was all light years away. He was roused from his daydreaming by someone calling his name. He turned to see Satomi and suddenly felt oddly embarrassed.

"Captain, come take a look at this."

Captain again... What the hell is it now? Taylor wondered, before moving up beside her to find out what merited the formality. She was looking at a tall black chamber, perhaps three meters high, one of a row of twenty that lined both sides of the room. "What's up?"

"These are stasis chambers," said Satomi.

Taylor's fingers tightened around the grip of his handgun. "Empty or occupied?"

"Occupied," said Satomi, but then she was quick to follow up with, "but malfunctioning; the unfortunate occupants of all twenty pods in this room are dead." Her speedy clarification was timely enough that Taylor didn't quick-draw his weapon.

Satomi reached up and wiped away the

condensation on the outside of the stasis chamber with the base of her fist, revealing the wizened, gnarled face of a dead Hedalt soldier. Taylor winced and recoiled.

"Hell's fire, how long has it been dead for?"

"That's the strange part," said Satomi, "the level of decomposition suggests it has been dead for at least a decade, perhaps a lot longer."

"What're you talkin' about? That'd mean it died before the war even started," said Blake, who had crept up behind Taylor and was scowling at the decayed Hedalt. Casey was behind him, looking slightly green.

"I know that, Blake, but I can assure you that the readings are correct." Satomi replied, cycling through the status readout on the chamber's console screen. "The stasis fields in these units all malfunctioned long before the revival cycles were triggered, which the data on this screen suggests only occurred a few days ago, maybe less. But..." she hesitated.

"I don't like 'buts'. But what, Satomi?" said Blake, sounding increasingly twitchy.

"But these stasis chambers aren't designed for extended hibernation. I'd say something went wrong that prevented the revival cycles from triggering at the proper time."

"What, so you're sayin' they were never supposed to be on ice for this long?" asked Blake, but then he frowned and added, "Just how long have these ugly SOBs been here for, anyways?"

Satomi was still peering at the data panel with narrowed eyes. "I can't tell exactly how long these chambers were in use for, but from what I can glean from the data, I'd say maybe a hundred years. Honestly, it could be a lot longer, it's impossible to be sure without more study."

"C'mon Satomi, are you sure?" said Blake, sounding increasingly irritated. "I mean, how can that be? You just ain't readin' it right, is all."

Satomi peered at Blake; her brow remained furrowed, but this time because she was cross, rather than confused, "Yes, I'm sure, Blake." she replied, testily, "and, yes, I'm reading it right."

Taylor thought for a moment, trying to make sense of their discoveries so far. He laid out the facts in his mind as plainly as he could. They had stumbled on a major Hedalt starship base, cleverly concealed in a lava tube in a distant arm of the galaxy so that no-one would find it, but one that had seemingly been abandoned long before the end of the war. In fact, if Satomi was correct then it was probable it had been abandoned long before the Hedalt war with Earth had even begun. But how and why were questions to which he had no answers. Why were these Hedalt put into stasis so long ago? Why build such a powerful military asset and not use it during the war with Earth? And if it had been intended as a reserve base – a sort of backup plan in case the war went badly for the Hedalt – why had they not returned to it when it was clear the Hedalt were on the losing side of the battle? From the limited information that Satomi had been able to gather, they knew the base could support at least twenty Hedalt Corvettes, and probably considerably more than that. It was firepower that could easily have turned the tide of the war against Earth. None of it made sense, and Taylor liked things to make sense. Then he remembered that there were five doors leading off the main corridor outside, and adrenalin kicked in again.

"Wait, Blake, you said there were three other rooms off the main corridor, just like this one?"

Blake nodded, "Yeah, that's right Cap..." and then realization dawned on him too. "Damn, there could be more of these chambers in those other rooms too!"

"Another hundred and twenty of them," added Casey, also recognizing the danger. "And maybe not all of them malfunctioned..."

"Let's move out, room to room, quick and clean," said Taylor, grabbing his sidearm and raising it to a high ready position. "Judging by the state of these chambers, it's likely the others will have malfunctioned too, but we can't afford to take any chances."

They cleared the room opposite, with Blake again on point, and then worked diagonally across. Both of the rooms were identical to the first, containing forty stasis chambers, all of which had been recently activated and all of which had malfunctioned decades earlier, killing the Hedalt occupants. Taylor began to feel more at ease, but there was still one room to go. They moved outside the final room and performed the same action again, conducted with the same polished proficiency. Blake went in first, as before, followed by Taylor, Satomi and then Casey.

"Clear!" Blake called out, "There's no one home and these chambers are all busted up, like the rest."

"Clear! Same here, Cap," called out Casey, and the relief was palpable in her voice.

"Clear... Mine are all dead too," Taylor followed, lowering the weapon to his side. "Looks like this base is a ghost, after all."

Then they all looked over at Satomi, waiting for her to confirm the all-clear, but her voice remained conspicuous by its absence, and Taylor felt a lump harden in his throat. He peered over to see Satomi standing by the final stasis pod in the row, staring up at it, her face white. Then she turned, met the eyes of Casey, followed by Blake and then Taylor. Even through her visor, Taylor could see that the little wrinkles at the sides of her eyes had tightened, a tell that he'd come to recognize over the years; one that meant she was scared, but trying to hold it together.

Satomi swallowed hard; her mouth was dry and her pulse was threatening to triple its usual, sedate resting rate. "Captain, this chamber is empty..."

NINE

Blake's head was on a swivel. He was alternating between peering up and down the corridor outside, through the window in the double doors, and glancing back at Satomi and the others in case there were any updates. Satomi continued to analyze the empty stasis chamber, trying to determine whether it had previously been occupied or had simply never been utilized to begin with. She scrolled through the information on the console screen, her face a furrowed mix of concern and concentration. Taylor watched her constantly, growing more anxious with each passing second, until Satomi deactivated the console and turned to him to make her report. It was short, and to the point.

"This pod was definitely active recently," said Satomi, "and by some miracle, it didn't malfunction like the others. It's safe to assume that there is at least one Hedalt soldier still active on the base."

Blake darted back into the room holding his handgun low in both hands, knuckles white. There was no need for him to state the worst-case scenario anymore, because they all knew it; all except Casey, who had anxiously folded her arms across her chest.

"But there's four of us, right?" Casey asked, directing the question towards both Taylor and Satomi. "Four versus one surely put the odds in our favor?" Casey had still been at the flight training academy when the war had ended, and so she had never seen action. Out of her five years in Earth Fleet, almost four of them had been spent in the near-solitude of their current DSR mission. For most of that time, she had been breezily lost in the vacuum, barely having to give a second thought to the real reason they were all out here. She would have to face it now.

"In space, fighting ship-to-ship, we can fly further and fight longer and harder than the Hedalt," responded Taylor, deciding the best way to tell her was without any sugar-coating. "Something about their physiology makes them poorly suited to space travel, but it's a different story fighting on the ground."

Blake moved next to Casey; he could see the fear behind her eyes, but, like Taylor, he knew the best way for Casey to survive was to be under no illusions as to what they were facing.

"They're animals, Casey. Down here, fightin' on the ground, one Hedalt soldier could take us all out."

Casey swallowed hard, but remained composed at least on the outside.

"Keeping the fight in space is how we won, Casey," added Satomi, "They are faster, stronger and tougher than us; they're born killers. But their Corvettes were no match for the Nimrods; that, and our crews could literally fly rings around them. It nullified their advantage of numbers. But, had the fight reached the ground, Earth would have surely fallen."

Casey's arms tightened further around her chest, as far as was possible given that, like the others, she was still wearing her environment suit. "Right..." then she took a deep breath, and looked embarrassed, as if she was about to own up to a dirty secret. She looked at Taylor directly, "You know, I... never really saw much fighting during the war, Cap. Actually, none at all."

Taylor smiled. "I know that, Casey, but you've had the same training as the rest of us, and I know I can count on you." Then he looked at Satomi and

Blake in turn, "I know I can count on all of you. We haven't just spent nearly four years in the darkest and coldest recesses of the galaxy only to die on this miserable lump of rock."

"I certainly ain't dyin' on a moon in the Scrotum-Crotch arm of the galaxy," said Blake, adding a welcome lightness, "and seein' as Casey's the only one who can fly us outta this rabbit warren, she sure as hell ain't dyin' here either. You hear me Casey?"

Casey managed a smile, "Your concern for my wellbeing is touching."

Blake laughed, "Don't knock it, Casey! If it came down to a choice between lettin' the Hedalt take you down or one of these two, I'm definitely savin' your ass. No offense, Captain."

"None taken," said Taylor, though he was only half-sure that Blake was kidding.

"Offense taken!" Casey hit back, thumping Blake on the arm of his suit. "I'm not some fairytale princess, Blake, I don't need rescuing, by you or anyone else. Besides, unless you sprout wings or learn how to pilot a Nimrod in the next few hours, it'll be me who does all the saving around here!"

Blake held up his hands in a mock gesture of surrender. "Whatever you say, Casey, just so long as you don't leave without me, is all."

"The thought never crossed my mind..."

"I suggest we remove our environment suits

and conceal them here," said Satomi, who was not in the mood for another saccharin exchange between Casey and Blake. "If there is a Hedalt soldier loose in this compound, these suits will only slow us down and make us easier targets."

Casey seemed shocked at the suggestion, "But, without the environment suits, we have no way of getting back to the ship?"

"We ain't getting' back to the ship until that Hedalt freak is dealt with," Blake cut in. "Satomi's right, we need to find that soldier an' take it out, before it finds us." Satomi was so surprised to hear Blake agree with her that she let out an involuntary laugh.

"How can you be sure it even knows we're here?" asked Casey.

"Between the watch tower outside an' Satomi helpfully switchin' on all the lights inside, I'm pretty sure it knows we're here, Casey."

Satomi glowered back at Blake; it hadn't taken long for him to get the daggers out again. The sardonic quip about turning the lights on was not meant playfully.

Taylor sensed Satomi's growing irritation and stepped in, "Look, we have no chance of fighting a Hedalt soldier if we're squabbling amongst ourselves," he said, looking at Blake, "so let's get out of these suits and find our unwanted friend as quickly as possible."

"Yes, Captain," said Satomi acidly, though she was still glowering at Blake who just stared back at her impassively, as if goading her on.

Taylor twisted his helmet and oxygen hissed out into the room as the seal was broken. He removed it and took a breath of the air in the room, which was cold and tasted stale and musty, like a damp cellar. He felt a chill run down his spine as the cold air replaced the warm air in his suit. Compared to the temperature-controlled environment of their ship the base felt positively arctic. He then turned towards Satomi while continuing to remove the rest of his environment suit.

"Satomi, once you're out of the suit, see if you can pull up a map of this complex and find us a place to source the parts we need."

Satomi removed her helmet and set it down on the ground, "Yes, sir. And I'll try to make sure I don't accidentally activate any other systems while I'm at it." She shot a snarky glance at Blake as she said this, but he was too busy removing his own suit to notice.

Unencumbered by the environment suit, and only wearing his regular uniform plus the combat body armor that Blake had assigned them all, Taylor almost felt like he was floating. They all stacked the suits next to the empty stasis chamber and then gathered behind Satomi, who had found a working computer console at the far end of the room.

"Have you got this place figured out yet?" asked Taylor, hopefully, rubbing his hands together to warm them up.

"I think so," Satomi replied, and then she stepped aside so the others could more clearly see the console screen. "As far as I can make out, we're here," she pointed to a room highlighted on a wire-framed, three-dimensional map displayed on the large screen. "This is one of two identical structures, possibly denoting two distinct combat wings. From the layout, I'd suggest we're just down from the main command and control center for the first combat wing. Living quarters and other non-combat structures seem to be over the other side of the lava tube, a good few kilometers from the operational part of the base."

"What's that?" asked Taylor, pointing to a large rectangular structure between their location and the other buildings on the opposite side of the cave.

"I'm not sure," replied Satomi, "but it looks like some sort of warehouse, or perhaps a factory. It's massive, though; it has to be at least a kilometer across each side."

"Maybe they intended to build the ships here too, but never got around to it?" suggested Casey.

"It's possible," agreed Taylor, massaging his

chin, glad that he was again able to do so. A self-contained shipyard and base, hidden from enemy eyes, would make a lot of sense, he mused. "But it's too far away to be of help to us, so let's focus on locations inside this structure that might have the kit we need." Then he pointed to one of the other sections on the map Satomi had found. "What's your best guess for these three areas?"

Satomi paused to consider the question, but Blake moved forward, barging into Satomi and causing her to glower at him again. "I'd put money on them bein' hangars Cap. I'd say there's likely to be fifteen or twenty ships in each."

"Agreed," said Satomi, jostling Blake back away from the screen. "Our best chance of finding either compatible RCS thrusters or the materials we need to fabricate them on the ship is to make our way there."

"Okay," said Taylor, still stroking his stubbled face, "that places these two sections in-between us and the closest hangar, if that's what they actually are." He pointed to a room, which appeared to be at the end of the corridor outside, and then to another similar-sized section next to that, leading on to what they guessed was the hangar. "We have to assume the Hedalt is hiding out somewhere in one of these sections."

"Hey, you never know, it might have already taken a ship and got the hell of this rock," suggested Casey, trying to remain optimistic. "Or it could have headed back to the other side of this lava cave, and be tucked up in bed in one of the accommodation blocks!"

"Hedalt don't sleep in beds like we do," said Satomi, missing the attempt at humor.

"I know that, Satomi," said Casey with more snark that anyone was used to hearing from her. "I'm just saying there's a good chance that it's not here anymore, that's all."

Casey had barely finished speaking when the lights in the room suddenly dimmed and the computer panel in front of them shut down.

"I somehow get the feelin' we ain't that lucky..." said Blake, before sprinting back to the door and prizing it carefully open to peer down the corridor again. "Hedalt eyes see better in low light levels than we do; this could mean it knows we're here and is coming for us."

"Or it could just be a power failure, Blake," Taylor added quickly, being the yang to his yin, "but, just in case it's not, let's be ready."

Blake waved them over, "Okay, c'mon, the corridor is clear."

"We move in twos," said Taylor as he reached the door. "Casey, you partner with Blake, and Satomi, you back me up."

Casey clenched the grip of her handgun and took a deep breath, "Aye, aye, Captain Taylor

Ray," she said, before moving up beside Blake, who gave her a soldierly rap on the shoulder with his fist.

He smiled at her and whispered, "Hey, he'll take any opportunity he gets to have her back him up, know what I mean?"

Casey shook her head and then returned his gesture of reassurance by thumping him gently on the chest, "That still doesn't make any damn sense, Blakey, but I love that you keep trying..."

"At the end of this corridor there's another double door," said Taylor, oblivious to Blake's continued failed attempts at innuendo. "We move up and then clear the room, nice and smooth, just like before."

"An' if you see anythin' movin' in there, you shoot it; ain't that right Cap?" added Blake, staring at Taylor with expectant eyes.

Ordinarily, Taylor would not countenance such a gung-ho approach, but on this occasion he couldn't dispute the logic. "Agreed, so long as the thing that's moving isn't one of us."

Blake moved out into the corridor first with Casey close behind, and then Taylor and Satomi followed, hugging the wall on the opposite side. Without their environment suits, they were able to move far more swiftly and also more quietly, but since the only other noise was the low hum of the dimmed overhead electric lights, every one of their footsteps still sounded like a hammer striking against the hard floor. They reached the door to the adjoining room and Taylor grasped the handle nodding to Blake, who raised his weapon and nodded back.

"On my mark. Three... Two... One... Go!"

TEN

Taylor yanked open the door so that the others could rush through, but instead of leading into another room or corridor the door opened onto a wide balcony, which surrounded and overlooked a multifaceted command and control center below. The simple wireframe map had not indicated the presence of the balcony and the unexpected setting temporarily threw Taylor off guard. He quickly surveyed the command center below, which was split into four sections, each of which provided ample opportunity for a Hedalt soldier to lay in wait for an ambush.

"Stay focused, everyone..." Taylor called out, trying to keep a lid on his volume level, despite the sudden flood of adrenaline. He moved further onto the balcony and stepped right to catch up with Satomi. Blake and Casey had swiftly moved left, but were still within earshot. "The soldier could be hiding anywhere in that lower level."

"I don't like this," Blake answered, "We're too exposed up here."

Satomi dropped to her knees, taking cover behind the glass balustrade that surrounded the balcony. "If Blake and Casey circle around counter-clockwise and check the other angles, we can then all meet up down by that corridor." She pointed towards the far right corner on the lower level and Taylor spotted the passageway that had been indicated on the wireframe map. He remembered that it led onto another room, perhaps a ready room or a briefing room. "If we move around in the other direction, it should make it impossible for anyone down there to stay hidden," Satomi continued.

"Okay, good plan, Satomi," said Taylor, dropping to a crouch beside her, while still keeping a watchful eye on the command center through the glass barrier. "Relay the instructions to Blake, but do it quietly; I'll cover you from here."

Taylor stood up and swept the barrel of his handgun over the balustrade, while keeping tabs on Satomi in his peripheral vision as she stayed low and hustled along the balcony towards Blake and Casey. Given their conspicuous earlier entrance onto the balcony, if the Hedalt soldier was hiding below then it would surely have been alerted to their presence. As such, he didn't want to risk just calling out the instructions to Blake, which could give the Hedalt the chance to overhear their plan.

Satomi had just reached Blake when a brief flicker of movement caught Taylor's attention; he aimed the weapon towards it and peered intently into the gloomy space below, his pulse quickening. He saw it again, just a hint of a shadow moving towards Satomi and the others, using the many consoles, desks and other items below as cover. Taylor slid his finger onto the trigger and steadied his breathing. He traced the path of the shadow and caught sight of it again. "Not so fast..." Taylor whispered and added pressure to the trigger, but before he could fire, light pulsed towards him from below and the glass balustrade shattered, showering his face with glass. He threw himself down and away from the edge, feeling the glass bite into his elbows and knees, as needle-like shards of purple energy slammed into the wall inches above his head, pockmarking the surface with singed holes the size of cherries. Taylor rolled to the side, wincing as the glass continued to slice into his thighs and arms – though the body armor at least protected his chest – and then pressed himself up, firing blindly in the direction of the shadow, but it had already moved. Shards of purple energy blinked up from the lower level again, but this time they were directed towards the others. The balustrade shielding them also shattered and he saw Satomi get hit in the chest and fall heavily.

"Satomi!" cried Taylor running towards her while again firing blindly at the shifting shadow of the Hedalt below, which ran into cover, before taking up a new position that blocked Taylor's line of fire. Blake took advantage of the opening and scrambled further around the balcony away from the others and also opened fire, while Casey dragged Satomi back from the edge. But the lull was short-lived as more plasma shards lashed the wall above their heads. Casey fired back, before the intensity of the incoming fire forced her to dive for cover too. Taylor landed beside Casey moments later and hurriedly checked Satomi for signs of injury. There were several smoldering holes in her body armor, but none of them appeared to have penetrated all the way through. There was also a small trickle of blood from where she'd hit her head on the balcony floor, but all things considered she did not seem seriously hurt. Relieved, Taylor rested his forehead on Satomi's shoulder and breathed a sigh of relief. As close calls came, it couldn't have been much closer.

"We have to concentrate our fire and drive it

back!" Taylor called to Casey over the searing roar of the Hedalt's plasma rifle as it continued to engage Blake, who was fighting tenaciously and without fear. He grabbed Satomi's weapon in his left hand and then steeled himself. "Are you ready?"

Casey nodded and shifted position, ready to leap up beside him. Taylor remembered her reticent earlier admission that she had never seen action, and was impressed at how coolly she was handling her first contact. She looked a hell of a lot more composed than Taylor felt, that much was certain.

Taylor jumped up with Casey at his side and both of them fired frantically towards the Hedalt, forcing it to retreat behind a low wall that separated a row of computer consoles from the adjacent walkway. Bullets rained down all around it and the Hedalt soldier let out a dull roar, before disappearing out of sight.

"You hit it!" Blake called out. There was excitement in his voice; for Blake, this was the thrill of the hunt. "It's hunkered down behind that partition; keep it suppressed, I have an idea!"

Taylor reloaded, fumbling his first attempt to slide in the new clip due to the adrenalin causing his hands to shake, and then frantically discharged his weapons towards the Hedalt's last known location. Bullets smashed through the computer consoles, causing them to spark and fizz like angry fireworks, but the thick partition wall continued to provide effective cover for their adversary.

"What are you going to do?" Taylor called out, glancing over at Blake, but he didn't need to hear an answer, because he could see Blake reloading his weapon with a bright red clip that had been stored in a pouch in his body armor. He was switching to experimental, explosive-tipped rounds.

Taylor's handgun clicked; he released the clip and reached for another, while Casey continued to fire, forcing the Hedalt to remain hidden. Taylor reloaded again and then saw Blake taking aim.

"Take cover, Casey!" he shouted, and then he ducked down behind a twisted section of the balustrade that hadn't already been obliterated by the Hedalt's previous onslaught.

Blake fired, but at the same moment the Hedalt darted across the back of the room, as if it had somehow sensed the impending danger. A cascade of small detonations disintegrated the partition wall and computer consoles where the Hedalt soldier had been moments earlier, kicking up thick plumes of acrid black smoke that filled the entire rear half of the control center.

Taylor sprang up and leant over what remained of the balustrade for extra support, searching for the Hedalt soldier, but the smoke had entirely obscured his view. If the Hedalt had survived the barrage, he had no way to know.

"Did you get it?" Casey called over to Blake, but her voice was drowned out by the crackling fires below. "I can't see anything!"

Suddenly the black cloud lit up from the inside with flashes of purple light and a burst of fire erupted from the darkness, obliterating the balcony supports underneath where Blake was standing and sending him crashing to the lower level in a mass of rubble, as if he'd been caught in an earthquake.

"Blake!" cried Casey, and she ran towards the collapsed section, firing randomly into the black cloud with one hand outstretched, until her clip was empty. Taylor also fired into the cloud, but then out of the corner of his eye he saw the Hedalt slip away down the corridor that the wire-framed map had suggested led towards one of the hangars. He covered the passageway in case the soldier re-emerged to chance another attack, but his gut told him the alien had fled to regroup in another location, where it would lie in wait to ambush them again.

"Blake! Where are you?!" Taylor heard Casey call out. She was standing at the edge of the collapsed balcony, peering down in the dust and rubble. Closer to him, he saw Satomi stir and then draw herself up to a sitting position, holding her head with one hand and pressing another to her chest, where the Hedalt weapon had almost penetrated. He rushed over and knelt at her side.

"Satomi, are you okay?"

"I think so," Satomi answered and then she tried to stand and it felt like needles were pressing into her chest. She halted half-way up and rested on her knees, pressing her fingers into the holes in her body armor. "What the hell hit me?"

"A Hedalt plasma rifle," said Taylor, "you're lucky to be alive."

Satomi then became aware of the two plumes of smoke; one from the explosive-tipped rounds that Blake had fired, and the greyer cloud of dust that was rising up from the pile of rubble where the balcony had collapsed, taking Blake along with it.

"What happened?" she said, with greater urgency.

"The Hedalt managed to slip away and Blake fell, I don't know if he's alive or dead."

"What? Where?"

"Can you stand?"

Satomi tried again to get up, but the effort shot more needles through her body. Taylor didn't wait for her to ask and helped her up, throwing her arm over his shoulder to take some of her weight.

"Help me to him," said Satomi; now that she was on her feet, she could see the full scale of the devastation for the first time and she feared the worst. Together, they hobbled along the balcony until they reached Casey's side.

"I can't see him!" Casey yelled, growing more frantic by the second, "We need to get down there."

"Okay, Casey, but we all go together," said Taylor, trying to keep his voice calm and level, "That soldier could be back any moment."

Taylor led the way back along the balcony and down the stairs on the wall opposite to where Blake had fallen. Satomi had regained some of her strength and was able to walk unaided again, and together with Casey they kept their weapons trained on the entrance to the corridor down which the Hedalt soldier had escaped. Taylor ran ahead and peeked down the passageway, seeing that the coast was clear.

"It's gone," said Taylor, edging out further into the corridor and keeping his weapon aimed down it. "Go and help Blake. Hurry!"

Casey ran to the pile of rubble and started clawing through it, pulling out jagged stones and crumpled metal as easily as if they were egg cartons. "Blake! Where are you?!" she shouted, "Call out to me, please!"

There was a weak shout and Casey clambered over the rubble towards it.

"Here... Casey, I'm... here."

Casey saw him, pressed beneath a girder,

which lay across his waist. "He's over here, help me!" she shouted back to the others, before dropping down beside him. Satomi was still several meters away, her injuries impeding her progress, while Taylor backed himself towards the rubble, keeping his weapon aimed along the corridor, just in case the Hedalt decided to make a sudden return.

"I need your help!" cried Casey, but Satomi and Taylor were still too far away, and she could see that the life was quickly ebbing away from Blake. Panic overwhelmed her, and with it came desperation. She had to do something; she had to try. She threw down her weapon and grasped the girder with both hands. Without thinking she lifted, screaming with exertion, like the ethereal cry of a banshee, wailing until the girder shifted and Blake managed to awkwardly slide out from under it. Taylor and Satomi finally arrived and hurried across the pile of rubble just in time to see Casey toss the girder aside and then collapse onto her back, panting for breath.

Satomi ran to attend to Blake, while Taylor dropped beside Casey and helped her into a sitting position, resting against the wall.

"How the hell did you manage that?" asked Taylor, glancing back at the enormous lump of metal that Casey had just tossed aside. He let out a giddy laugh, a mix of surprise and fear, and then looked back at his pilot. Casey was lithe and strong like a dancer, but it should have taken ten Casey's to lift the mass she had just heaved off Blake by herself. "Have you been hiding superpowers from me all this time?"

"I... don't know, Cap..." said Casey smiling, but still gasping for air. "I just... did it. But now my arms feel like they're going to fall off."

"Well, make sure they don't," said Taylor, and he found himself automatically looking at her arms to check they weren't actually hanging loose by threads of tissue and tendons. "We need you and your arms to fly us out of here, remember?"

Casey let her head flop back against the wall and closed her eyes. She felt like she'd just run a marathon, "Aye, aye, Captain Taylor Ray."

"Captain, I need you now..." said Satomi, calmly but with firmness.

Captain again... Taylor thought, and his gut churned, expecting the worst. He left Casey resting and joined Satomi, but it was only then that he saw the extent of the injuries to Blake. Cuts, bruises and even breaks could be fixed easily, but without the medical bay on the ship, there were limitations to what they could do in the field, and they were certainly not equipped to deal with serious trauma.

"We're looking at multiple rib fractures, probable flail chest, and a massive hemothorax," said Satomi in a hushed voice, "I think also a punctured lung, and a number of other internal injuries that I can't assess without getting him back to the ship."

"Hey, don't talk like I'm not here..." said Blake weakly. His breath was rapid and shallow and his skin had turned pale and clammy. "Just tell me straight; am I gonna die?"

Satomi looked at Taylor and her eyes both implored him for help and told him the answer to Blake's question at the same time. Taylor knew Satomi well enough to be able to determine her answer from the lines around her eyes and the way her chin tightened. Blake was dying and there was nothing she could do about it.

"Don't look at him..." said Blake, struggling harder to breathe, "Satomi, just tell me, please. I'd rather the truth than you string me along."

Satomi looked down, "Yes," she said softly, "I'm so sorry, Blake."

Blake coughed and then reached out and took Satomi's hand. His grip was weak. "It's okay, Satomi, it ain't your fault."

Satomi managed to raise her gaze just enough to look into Blake's eyes. He smiled at her and squeezed her hand again, though Satomi barely felt the increase in pressure.

"We can try to stabilize you and make you more comfortable," said Taylor, sensing that Blake did not have long left. "We'll stay with you."

They were all silent for a moment, save the sound of the raspy, shallow breaths coming from Blake. Then Blake closed his eyes and shook his head, so gently that the gesture was almost imperceptible.

"No, don't stay," said Blake between raspy breaths, "I don't want Casey to know."

Taylor understood where Blake was going, but he didn't like it. Deceiving Casey now would only delay her pain, and ultimately make it more acute.

"She needs to know, Blake..." Taylor began, but Blake reached out with his other hand and managed to grab Taylor's body armor, and with excruciating effort pull him closer.

"No, not now. It'll kill her too," said Blake, spitting blood onto his chin and lips. "Wait till you're safe. Wait till that bastard Hedalt is dead. Just tell her..." he paused and seemed to wane out of consciousness for a moment before coming to again. "Just tell her I'm gonna be okay. Tell her you've medded me up, but that you have to leave me here. She'll believe it comin' from you, Cap. You know she will."

"Blake, I don't think we should lie..." Taylor began, but Blake just wrestled him closer, his face contorting with pain as he did so.

"Don't tell her, you hear me? Just kill that alien scumbag and get the hell off this rock."

Taylor glanced back at Casey; she was still resting with her eyes closed. The exertion of lifting the girder had seemingly wiped her out. He looked back into Blake's eyes and then grabbed his hand and squeezed it tightly.

"Okay, Blake, I won't tell her," he assured him, "but that's because we're not giving up. Satomi will do what she can to fix you up, and then you just hang on, you hear me? Hang on, and we'll come back for you with the medevac gear once we get back to the ship."

Blake attempted to laugh, but his chest spasmed and he coughed more blood onto his chin, "Hell, Taylor, I always did admire your optimism."

"Just do it, that's an order," said Taylor, his voice as grave a Blake's condition. Then he turned to Satomi and with more sensitivity, added. "Do what you can, Satomi. I'm going to check out what's at the other end of that corridor, and try to figure out our next move."

Taylor tried to stand, but Satomi caught him by the front of his body armor, her hand covering the bloody mark left behind by Blake. "Be careful, Taylor," she said, fixing him with wide eyes, "That's an order."

Taylor smiled, "You got it, boss. Don't worry."

Satomi's grip remained and it felt almost as if she was trying to pull him closer, but then her eyes narrowed and her expression hardened, and she released him. She held his eyes for a second longer, as if there was something more she wanted to say, before turning back to her patient.

Taylor took a fresh clip of armor-piercing rounds from the pouch on his body armor and slowly slid down over the rubble towards Casey. Her eyes opened narrowly as he approached and she lifted her head off the wall.

"How's he doing, Cap?" asked Casey. Her tone was hopeful, which made the lie that Taylor needed to tell all the more painful to bear.

"He's pretty beat up, Casey, but he's going to be okay," said Taylor. He must have sounded convincing because Casey smiled.

"That's good to hear."

"Satomi is stabilizing him, and then we'll come back for him later, with the medevac gear."

Casey's smile fell off her face and she pushed herself up, but Taylor caught her, placing a hand on her shoulder and gently halting her advance.

"Woah, not so fast, Casey."

"But Captain, we can't just leave him here," Casey protested. "I should stay with him."

"He told me you'd say that, Casey," replied Taylor, improvising and also compounding the lie with more lies. "but we need you to help take out that soldier. That's our best way to help Blake now, Casey, do you understand?"

Casey glanced across to where Satomi was tending to Blake, and then back to Taylor. She rested back against the wall and gently patted Taylor's hand, which was still on her shoulder, "Aye, aye, Captain Taylor Ray."

Taylor smiled and released his hold on her, "Thanks, Casey. We'll be back in no time." Casey nodded hesitantly and shut her eyes again. Taylor took the opportunity to leave, feeling sick to his stomach and ashamed. Blake may have been right, but the deception would leave a scar that would never heal, because Casey would not get the chance to say goodbye. She might forgive Blake for that, in time, but whether she would forgive him for his complicity he did not know. Perhaps it was selfish to think of himself, but the trust of his crew mattered more to Taylor even than the mission, and he couldn't bear it if Casey felt less of him as a result.

Taylor skidded down the last of the rubble and stalked towards the last-seen location of the Hedalt soldier. He reached the corridor and waited, listening intently for any indication of movement, but there was only a deathly silence, punctuated by the occasional crack of a broken electrical system and click of a malfunctioning overhead light. He glanced back towards where Satomi and the others were still concealed behind the rubble of the wrecked balcony and then made a decision that he knew was stupid, but resolved to follow through with anyway. He would go after the Hedalt alone to ensure no-one else got hurt. They were his crew and his responsibility. They were only two weeks away from the end of their mission; two weeks away from when they should be heading home with enough pay for them all to start new lives. Blake would not make it back, and he wouldn't let Satomi or Casey share his fate. He had insisted that they take on this mission, because rules were rules and the mission came first. But none of them deserved to die on an unknown rock twenty thousand light years from Earth. And he sure as hell wasn't going to die here, either.

ELEVEN

Taylor edged around the corner at the end of the long passageway, weapon raised in readiness, and glanced into the adjoining space. According to the basic schematic that Satomi had found in the computer system, this new area should lead on to one of three possible hangars, hopefully containing the equipment they needed. But, first, the threat of the Hedalt soldier had to be dealt with.

As Taylor crept further inside, he could see that the space was split into two sections, one of which resembled a small lecture theater, with glass walls, while the remainder of the room had a more casual layout, with seating areas and a variety of different breakout spaces that he couldn't properly identify the purpose of due to the dim lighting. As he stepped cautiously inside, he found his mind wandering and exploring extraneous thoughts, such as the strangeness of seeing chairs and tables, since he'd never imagined a Hedalt to sit in the same way humans did. Then again, he'd never been inside a Hedalt base quite like this, so everything he was seeing was new. He tried to focus on more useful thoughts, and surmised that it was perhaps a combined briefing room and ready room, which if true would mean that the hangar and flight deck would lead on from it, increasing the odds of finding salvageable parts to repair their ailing Nimrod-class cruiser.

He checked the area contained within the glass walls first, finding it empty. In fact, Taylor could find no evidence that it had ever been populated or used in anger. Other than the dust, it seemed untouched. He moved back outside, cautiously sticking to the walls as much as possible. Unlike the command center, the ready room, if that was its purpose, was open-plan and contained few places to hide or launch an ambush from, and Taylor was diligent in ensuring that any such nooks and crannies were thoroughly checked. The Hedalt had got the jump on him once already; not again.

The door to the hangar lay ahead and he crept slowly towards it, but then his foot slipped forward and he had to react quickly to stop himself from falling. Crouching down, he noticed a liquid shimmering on the bare metal deck plating. He touched it and rubbed it between his fingers; it was thick and dark. *Hedalt blood...* he realized. He stayed low and scoured the deck for other traces of the substance, quickly spotting a thin trail leading to the exit doors into what he assumed would be the hangar. He tightened his grip on the handgun and followed the path traced by the blood up to the door, noticing as he got closer that there was more blood on the handle. He took several deep breaths, placed his hand next to the bloody mark left by the Hedalt soldier and then pushed though.

His heart was beating faster than the movement of his hands, as he checked right then left, and then dashed for cover behind a stack of storage containers. He'd half-expected to be shot or clubbed around the head the moment he had sprung through the doors, but his gamble had paid off, this time. He peeked around the side of the containers to get a better view and it quickly became apparent that their assumptions had been correct; this was indeed a Hedalt starship hangar. It was huge. Taylor could see rows of Hedalt Corvettes lined up, side-by-side and as he counted the ones he could see without breaking out from his position of cover he calculated that Blake's estimate had been on the money. There were perhaps fifteen or twenty Corvettes inside, though the hangar could accommodate considerably more. But just one of the Hedalt vessels would be sufficient in order to salvage the components needed to fabricate new RCS thrusters in their ship's workshop.

Like the other parts of the base, the hangar looked both ancient and also as if it had never been used. Stacks of containers, like the ones he was hiding behind, lined the rear of the hangar, behind each ship that he could see. Whether they were supplies that had been intended to be loaded onto each Corvette , or just equipment for the hangar, Taylor couldn't be certain, but they would provide the cover he needed to approach the closest Corvette, hopefully undetected.

The next nearest stack of containers was about twenty meters away, a distance he could cover in a matter of seconds if he moved quickly enough, but if the Hedalt was hidden somewhere inside, lying in wait, it would also provide it with ample opportunity to execute another ambush. Taylor took a deep breath and got ready to run, tensing every muscle in his body so that he was like a coiled snake, ready to strike. Then he sprang forward and made a dash for the second stack of containers, but he barely made it five meters before the air was ignited by purple bolts of energy, which seared the deck plating all around him. It was either poor aim, perhaps due to the Hedalt's injuries, or sheer fluke, but Taylor somehow managed to not get hit, and as he dropped behind the second stack of containers, he knew he was lucky that his prideful and reckless actions hadn't got himself killed. *Let's hope fortune does truly favor the bold, and that I'm not just fortune's fool...* he thought.

His musings were interrupted by shards of energy lashing into the containers above his head, showering him with sparks. He pressed back against the metal boxes as two more bolts seared past, before the firing abruptly stopped. He tried to catch his breath, but his heart was thumping like a frenzied boxer and his arms and legs fizzed with adrenalin. He hadn't seen where the Hedalt had fired from, but the angle at least put it in the first quarter of the hangar, assuming it had not immediately moved after firing. He peeked around the side of the containers and a bolt flashed past his face, close enough that he could feel the heat on his skin.

Damn, it Taylor, think! he scolded himself, while ducking deeper into cover behind the containers, several of which were now either on fire or melting. He was in a bad spot; he couldn't retreat back through the door into the ready room without risking being shot at again, and he doubted his chances of being able to get an accurate shot off at the Hedalt before a plasma shard seared through his chest.

"Come on, think, there must be an option!" Taylor roared, this time out-loud in case hearing the words in his own ears would trigger his brain to come up with a solution. Then he looked up and noticed that the topmost containers were high enough to allow for an elevated view across the entire hangar. If he climbed to the top, he might be able to spot the Hedalt soldier, and possibly even get a shot off at it, before it realized where he was. It was risky, but as more purple energy bolts thumped into the containers two meters from his location, he decided there wasn't really a choice.

"Satomi is going to kill me for doing this..." he told himself, as he started to climb up the dense stack of containers, which wobbled precariously as he rose higher. Weapons fire from the soldier continued to flash all around him, but all of it was focused at ground level; the Hedalt had evidently not assumed that Taylor was stupid enough to scale a tower of burning and melting containers.

He reached the top and stole a look over the edge. Bolts of energy lashed towards him, but still aimed low. The Hedalt hadn't seen him; not yet. He leopard-crawled forward, handgun still gripped tightly in his grasp, until he was able to see down into the hangar below. He stretched out the weapon and aimed into the space ahead, waiting for the Hedalt to fire and give away its position; it duly obliged. Taylor traced the bolts back to the source and saw the soldier, perched on the wing of one of the Hedalt Corvettes, using its hull for cover and the advantage of elevation to gain a better viewpoint, exactly as it had done for Taylor.

"Now I've got you!" said Taylor and he squeezed the trigger, unleashing a controlled burst of armor-piercing rounds towards the Hedalt's position. His shots landed wide, but penetrated into the metal of the ship's wing, just close enough to force the soldier to withdraw. Taylor saw it slip and then dangle precariously from the edge of the wing before falling just out of his view. It would have been a controlled fall of perhaps two or three meters; not enough to kill it, but certainly enough to wind it and, hopefully, make it think twice about pressing its attack.

Taylor pushed himself up into a kneeling position, craning his neck in an attempt to reacquire his target, and then he saw it stagger out from underneath the cruiser and take cover next to a maintenance station. Taylor fired again and the rounds from his powerful weapon penetrated through the station and forced the Hedalt to scurry from cover, firing blindly in his direction. At times like these you need luck on your side, but the roll of the dice had not gone Taylor's way. He watched as the bolts of energy seemed to approach him in slow motion, and as he twisted his body away from the approaching shards, he felt the containers beneath him give way and collapse. The sensation of falling was brief and terrifying, and was followed by the crushing agony of his head hitting the deck.

TWELVE

There was a flash of brilliant, white light and Taylor found himself standing on the balcony of an apartment overlooking a great river. It felt familiar, but also completely alien. He was resting on the balcony with a glass in his hand containing about an inch of amber liquid. He smelt it then took a sip, and the smooth vanilla finish of the whiskey was vividly familiar, yet it also felt like the first time he'd ever tasted it.

He heard voices and spun around, spilling his drink in the process, to see Satomi, Casey and Blake sitting and chatting at a table behind him. They looked strange, as if a thin rubber sheet had been stretched across their faces. They suddenly stopped talking and looked at him, before raising their glasses. Taylor opened his mouth to speak, but they vanished, then the balcony, river and everything else melted away, and he was again surrounded by an intense white light that should have been blinding, yet it did not hurt his eyes.

There was the sensation of falling again, and then his feet hit metal and the white light fizzled away, as if there had been a spotlight shining in his face that had just been switched off. His eyes adjusted and he instantly recognized that he was on the bridge of a Nimrod-class cruiser, sitting in the command chair, though he couldn't be certain that it was his ship. The other stations were occupied, but instead of Casey in the pilot's chair, the seat was occupied by someone he did not recognize; a sort of faceless mannequin. He looked at the tactical station and then the mission operations station and both were occupied by similar-looking humanoid mannequins that appeared to have no discernable age or gender, or any distinguishing features that could tell one apart from another.

The viewport switched on, showing the predatory shape of another Nimrod-class cruiser bearing down on then. *No, wait, not a Nimrod...* Taylor realized, suddenly conflicted despite initially being certain of what he was seeing. *It's a Hedalt Corvette. Or is it?* The confusion was short-lived as the heads of the faceless mannequins all spun towards him like they were possessed and cried out in chorus, "Captain, what do we do?" Taylor was too much in shock to answer, and then they chorused again, "Captain, they're firing at us!" Taylor saw the flash from the enemy vessel's cannons and the whole ship shook as the shells slammed into the hull. The viewport exploded, followed by each of the three main consoles – pilot, tactical, mission ops – leaving the faceless mannequins burning lifelessly at their stations, like Guy Fawkes effigies on a bonfire. Taylor screamed and tried to run to help them, to pull them out of the flames, but for some reason he could not move his feet. The ship was rocked again by pulses of energy and alarms sounded all around him.

"Abandon ship!" Taylor ordered, and then he had a dread sense of déjà vu. He looked down at the console screen in his command chair and could see that the hull was breached in several locations and that their main reactor core was damaged. He knew the ship was dead in space; he'd been here before.

"Abandon ship!" he cried out again, "The Hedalt have attacked. Send a signal to Earth Fleet Command, the Hedalt have attacked. It's war!"

The bridge of the ship seemed to crumble around him and Taylor had the sensation of being thrown into the air. Then he was falling again and he felt himself slipping into darkness, but it was not the same as unconsciousness. He pressed his eyes shut, expecting to crash into the deck of the bridge at any moment, but then the falling stopped, and everything was still and quiet.

He opened his eyes and discovered that he was lying prone, but instead of his face being pressed against the cold, silver metal decking of a starship's bridge or the Hedalt hangar deck, he was lying on a pure black surface that felt unlike anything he'd touched before. It had no texture or temperature, and it felt neither hard nor soft, yet it resisted the press of his body. It was as if it wasn't there at all, yet it prevented him from falling further into the darkness that now enveloped him.

He pressed his hands to the surface and pushed himself up. He was in a corridor with black walls and a black ceiling constructed from the same impossible black material that he had woken up on. *Am I awake? Am I in a coma? What the hell is this place?* These and other questions invaded his mind, but all of them were equally unanswerable.

He stepped forward a few paces and his footsteps made no sound, despite the obvious sensation of his boots stepping on something solid enough to oppose his weight.

"Hello?" he called out, but his voice vanished into the darkness without any echo or reverberation as if he was standing at the peak of a mountain and his breath had been swallowed whole by the wind. "Hello, is there anybody here?" he called out again, but the words vanished as before, and there was no answer. He felt panic and terror start to swell inside his gut, but he fought back his primal fight-or-flight instincts. *Come on Taylor, hold it together...*

He continued to move cautiously forward, and the corridor seemed to grow and stretch out in front of him endlessly. Taylor quickened his pace as panic again threatened to overwhelm him, but then out of the darkness a door formed, bright and sharply-defined against the blackness, like a star in the deepest, clearest night.

He moved up to it, but there was no handle. He tried pushing the door, but though his hands landed on the surface and he felt it push back against his weight, like the floor beneath his feet, there was no sensation of texture and it was neither hot nor cold.

Taylor spun around and pressed his back to the door. The shock and strangeness of his new environment had initially dulled his senses, but despite his efforts to control his emotions, his mind was now fully giving in to fear.

"What is this place?" he shouted out. "Is there anyone here? Help me! Somebody, please help me!"

He ran away from the door, back the way he had come, but the corridor just stretched out endlessly in front of him, as before. He stopped, feeling breathless and giddy, and spun around again. The starlight door had disappeared and now he was surrounded only by an oppressive darkness that seemed to be pressing in on him. He screamed, but then without warning the walls, floor and ceiling of the corridor seemed to change and become opaque, and he was surrounded by pinpricks of light and swirling clusters of gas. The sense of vertigo was intense and Taylor fell to one knee, feeling dizzy and nauseous.

The disorientation passed quickly and he was able to stand again and take in his new surroundings, and as he looked all around, above and below, he suddenly realized what he was looking at. He was standing in space, encircled by stars and nebulae and galaxies, but also strangely removed from it all, as if he was looking through Casey's pilot's viewport. But this was not a virtual reality; it was too pristine, too perfect for that. This was something else.

He continued along the corridor, the surfaces of which were still faintly visible, like looking through thick glass, feeling calmer, despite his predicament not having improved. And then, out of the starlit darkness ahead of him the door appeared again, bright and flawless, but just as impassable as before.

Taylor considered trying to kick down the

door, as it seemed to be the only way in or out of wherever he was, but as he stepped back, readying himself to launch his boot at the door's center, he heard a sound. He stopped and listened and heard it again; it was the sound of someone shouting, but from where he could not tell. The cry came again and surrounded him from every direction.

"Who is it?" Taylor shouted into the darkness, but the voice didn't respond. "Who's there?" he tried again, but there was no answer and his voice just vanished into oblivion as it had done before.

Suddenly, the pin-pricks of starlight all around him started to diminish, and the swirling galaxies and nebulae faded to nothing. Taylor twirled around, looking up and down, but it was the same in every direction. The brilliant starlight door was all that remained, until that too faded into nothing, and Taylor was once again consumed by a crushing darkness, terrified and alone. He tried calling out again, but although his mouth moved, no sound came out.

This is it... he thought, gravely. *This is the end. This is what death is like.*

Then the darkness transformed into brilliant light and he was falling again, but this time when he landed he felt the thud of his body striking metal. He felt the coolness of its touch and detected the dimples in the surface of the deck plating. He felt the cool air of the hangar base against his face, though he did not feel cold. He felt all this, yet his body felt no pain from the impact of the fall, despite him hitting the deck like a butchered carcass. But although his body was numb, his head raged as though a volcano had erupted inside his skull, paralyzing him. And then, just as suddenly as the dark gulag had vanished, the pain was gone.

THIRTEEN

The shouting grew louder and more distinct and then Taylor was aware of the sound of weapons firing. But he could only discern the crack of Earth Fleet sidearms; the vibrant pulse of the Hedalt Plasma rifle was strangely absent. *The Hedalt soldier!* He realized. *Casey and Satomi must be fighting it!*

The dazzling, white light began to fade and his vision started to clear. He was lying on his back in the hangar bay, buried beneath a pile of containers, but although they pushed heavily against his body, and he could feel the pressure of their touch, he felt no pain. He tried to concentrate his gaze towards the sound of shouting and gunfire, but his eyes still struggled to focus and the blurry images that he could resolve appeared grainy, like an old photograph that was taken when the light level was too low.

He drew breath and felt the air enter his mouth, but there was no sensation of his lungs filling or his chest expanding. Then he realized he couldn't feel his heart beating and panic gripped him. He lay still again, petrified that his injuries were so severe that shock had already deadened him to the pain that his body must be silently enduring. Yet, as he lay motionless, wracked with a sense of dread that his body was broken and dying, his pulse did not quicken – in the same way that he was unaware of his heartbeat, he also could not feel the thud of blood pulsating in his neck. The terror that Taylor was experiencing should have been accompanied by a nauseating tightening of the gut, but he felt no such reaction from his own body; it was only his mind that had descended into the anarchy of fear. But while his body seemed detached, it was not numb; he could still feel the textured metal of the deck and detect the sharp corners of the containers pressing against him, and he could still feel the cool, still air against his face. Somehow, he could feel the world around him, but only partially. It was like a bizarre kind of anesthetic, which left him conscious of external stimulation, but dead to pain and any primal, physical manifestations of emotion.

The shouting and weapons fire continued to reach his ears, clearer and more distinct with each passing second, but he remained too afraid to move; too afraid to check himself over for fear of what he might discover. But then he heard what sounded like Satomi's voice, shouting for Casey to take cover, followed by more harrowed cries of, "Move right!"... "There it goes!"... "Watch out!"... and he knew he had to set aside his doubts and help, even if his dying body could do no more than offer the Hedalt soldier an additional target.

He placed his hands against the containers that lay on his chest and pushed; remarkably, they lifted and he was able to throw them to one side with ease and climb up onto his knees without any difficulty or sensation of pain. His vision was getting sharper, but it still looked like he was seeing the world through a malfunctioning viewport. In the days before ocular correction, they would have called it being 'short sighted'. Despite the fuzziness, he could make out his weapon resting on the deck a few meters ahead; he crawled to it and clutched it in his hand, before looking up and trying to get his bearings. His eyes didn't need their full resolution to recognize the muzzle flash of a weapon being fired, and he rose up and ran towards it, without any consideration as to the danger it might place him in. He could only think of Satomi and making sure she didn't end up like Blake; dead on a barren world on the other side of the galaxy.

He could make out the shapes more clearly now and headed towards a maintenance station with what should have been one of the many Hedalt Corvettes, but as he got closer he skidded to a halt and stared up at the ship in astonishment. *How can that be?* he asked himself, peering up at the ship and squinting, trying to force his eyes to focus, though it made no difference. Even though he could not see it sharply, he could see well enough that the vessel was clearly not a Hedalt Corvette, but a Nimrod-class cruiser. It was an Earth Fleet ship. Taylor remained frozen to the spot, crippled with questions. *Is it my ship? Has the Hedalt brought it inside the hangar? But when and why? Or was this always here? No, I would have seen it!*

His thoughts were interrupted by the metallic chime of a round ricocheting off the deck plating to his side. Instinctively he ran for cover behind the maintenance consoles as more rounds landed close by. *Who the hell is shooting at me?* he asked himself, considering that perhaps the Hedalt soldier had damaged its plasma rifle and had somehow managed to take either Casey's or Satomi's weapon instead. But if that was true, it meant one of them was injured; maybe already dead. Either way, he was running out of time.

Taylor's mind was still spinning, but his eyes had recovered enough that he was able to take stock of his environment, and what he saw next did nothing to calm the whirlwind in his head. Peering down along the full length of the hangar he saw, lined up like fossils in a museum, three entire squadrons of Nimrod-class cruisers. The Hedalt Corvettes had all gone. He considered whether he could have somehow stumbled into a different hangar, or perhaps fallen so hard that he'd crashed through the deck and landed on a lower level. But such a fall would have surely killed him. Or perhaps the blow to his head had been so severe that he was suffering from hallucinations. The crack of weapons fire again wrestled him from his contemplations.

"Taylor, is that you!?" he heard Satomi cry, though her voice seemed strange. He tried to see her, but his view was blocked, and he didn't want to expose his already battered head to a potential bullet from the Hedalt soldier's stolen weapon. "If you're there then move!" Satomi continued, "it's coming for you, Taylor, you have to..." then her words were cut short and the repeated *crack, crack, crack* of a handgun firing replaced the end of her sentence. Taylor shuffled around the maintenance console and began to work his way to the rear, but then a small, but highly-focused explosion rattled the deck and forced him to backtrack. *That was an explosive-tipped round! Satomi, what the hell are you doing?*

"Satomi, switch back to armor piercing, before you blow us all to hell!" he called out, but like Satomi's voice, his own words sounded strange to his ears, and he shook his head to try to clear the fogginess. "Satomi, do you hear me? You'll blow the fuel containers and this whole place will go up!" His voice still sounded different, wrong somehow, but since this was just another one of a number of baffling incongruities, he set it aside and waited for Satomi's reply, which did not come. Fearful that she had been hit, he continued to edge his way around the maintenance console. He glanced over to where Satomi's explosive-tipped rounds had punched a hole in the hangar deck, making sure that the Hedalt soldier was not using the smoke from the smoldering cavity as cover to flank him. But then through the haze he caught sight of a body on the deck and froze. It was a human woman.

"Satomi!" he cried out and ran towards the prone woman, ignoring the obvious danger of being shot, and slid to his knees beside her. Hastily holstering his weapon, he reached down and nervously turned the woman's head to face his, apprehensive of confirming his worst fears. But, incredibly, the face he looked down on was not Satomi's, and nor was it the face of Casey Valera.

The feeling of relief was like waking from a horrific nightmare and realizing that it was just a dream. He closed his eyes and breathed a hollow sigh of relief, though as before there was no sensation of his lungs filling or emptying and his body remained disconnected from the tumult of emotions he was enduring. Nevertheless, the action of sighing somehow still soothed his mind.

Able to think more clearly, the next question assaulted him like a club to the head. *Wait, if this is not Satomi or Casey, then who the hell is it?* He again peered down at the woman and his eyes narrowed and his brow furrowed. The muscles in his face felt stiff, as if his cheeks and eyebrows had been injected with a firming agent of the sort that was popular with those trying to regain the youthful look of their earlier years. But even this sensation was not as strange as the sight of the unknown woman before him. *Where did you come from and what the hell are you doing, over twenty thousand light years from Earth?*

She was middle-aged, perhaps forty, and tall, with mousy hair that was hanging across a square face, covered in grime and dried blood. She was curled into a fetal position, and her shoulder appeared to be bleeding from a superficial wound, but otherwise she looked fit and strong.

"Who are you?" Taylor asked the woman, who was beginning to stir.

"Captain, what are you doing?!"

Taylor shot around, suddenly remembering about the Hedalt soldier. With the rash of crazy events that had occurred over the past few minutes, he had lost all sense of what was happening around him.

"Captain, move away!"

The source of the voice was Satomi, and though she was standing just far enough away from Taylor's blurry eyes for her to appear indistinct, it was clear she was pointing her weapon at him. Behind Satomi was another figure, who appeared even blurrier. *Is that Casey?* Taylor thought, but if it was then she was unarmed and appeared to be hunched over; perhaps injured.

"Has the Hedalt soldier been killed? Did you get it?" Taylor called over to her.

"What are you talking about?" said Satomi, still pointing the weapon at him. She sounded incredulous. "You know it has!"

Her reply made no sense. Why would she assume he already knew? But, it was just another of the many questions that would have to wait, because the mysterious woman on the floor needed medical attention. "Then put down the damn weapon and get over here, she's hurt."

Satomi stepped forward, which helped Taylor to resolve her features more clearly, but instead of rushing to the woman's aid, she looked behind at the second figure.

"Captain, Casey has a broken arm and is pretty cut up, but she'll be okay..." Satomi answered, but she was speaking the words to him like he was mad. Then her mood darkened, as if Taylor had become the enemy. "Captain, you're starting to really scare me; what the hell are you doing?"

Taylor's frown deepened to a scowl. "I don't mean Casey for pity's sake, I mean the woman right here on the deck! Can't you see her?" He again looked down at the woman to check that he wasn't actually going mad, and he saw that her eyes had now opened and that she was watching him back, rapt with terror. He turned back to Satomi, but now that she was closer he could see that she looked strange, like her face had been smoothed over with a thin layer of clay. Nothing was making sense.

"Captain, I need you to step away from it," said Satomi, now aiming the weapon at the woman.

"What the hell are you doing? Put that down!" shouted Taylor; anger was overtaking confusion as his driving emotion. "I order you to help her now!"

"Captain, that's the Hedalt soldier..."

"What?" He swung back to the woman, who was now alert and trying to push away from him. "This is a woman; a human woman. Can't you see? What the hell is going on?!"

Before Satomi could answer, the woman

snatched Taylor's handgun from its holster and jolted upright, and before Taylor could process what had happened, two shots rang out cleanly in the otherwise icy stillness of the hangar.

FOURTEEN

Satomi collapsed forwards and slammed into the deck like a felled tree. Taylor released a primal, alien-sounding cry and rushed to her side, turning her over onto her back, but her body felt rigid, as if it had been flash-frozen. Bullet holes were clearly visible in her body armor, but there were more than could be explained by just the two shots that Taylor had seen the mysterious woman fire. Stranger still, the burn holes from when she had been hit by the Hedalt soldier's plasma rifle were no longer visible. He pressed his hands over the holes as best he could, instinctively trying to stem the flow of blood, but there was no blood. Muddled and still in shock, he looked up, but instead of peering into Satomi's kind, chestnut eyes, he saw something unreal staring back at him. He jolted away from the body, repulsed by it. It was just like in his dream; the mannequin. Except this mannequin had silver eyes and a single bullet hole in its forehead.

"No, please no! She can't be dead!" The voice was Casey's, but Taylor didn't look at her; he was still reeling from what he'd just seen, unsure if it was real or another hallucination. Perhaps he was even in a coma, and this was just a cruel trick that his battered and unconscious mind was playing on him.

"Stay back, Casey," Taylor ordered, "we don't know what this woman will do next."

"Captain, what woman?" cried Casey, on the verge of tears. "What is going on with you?!"

Taylor didn't answer and climbed to his feet. His eyes, now sharply in focus, were fixed on the woman who had just shot Satomi Rose. She was steady on her feet now, weapon aimed at his chest, but she was also studying him with a mix of fear and fascination, as if Taylor were an alien species that she was laying eyes upon for the first time. He glanced back down at the body again, and saw the mannequin-like facsimile of Satomi staring blankly up through alien silver orbs. Shock was curdling into rage. What had this woman done to her? Fury engulfed his mind, and though his body did not experience a rush of adrenalin, his anger felt as real as anything he'd ever felt before.

"What are you?" the woman shouted.

Taylor gritted his teeth and stormed towards her like a frenzied bull, but the attack was clumsy and easy to avoid. He felt the butt of the handgun whip him across the face and he stumbled and dropped to one knee, but again there was no pain; just a detached sensation of the impact.

"Do that again and I'll destroy you," the woman warned, menacingly, watching Taylor like a hawk, while also keeping half an eye on Casey, who was frozen, staring down at the inert mannequin of Satomi. The woman's next words were strangely softer and more hopeful, "I need you to tell me what you see."

Taylor remained on one knee and glanced up at the woman, who he now realized was wearing an Earth Fleet uniform, adorned with the rank of Commander. It was one absurdity too many and Taylor could feel his resolve ebbing away. *Too many questions. I can't take this anymore...* The anger began to bleed out from his mind, like wine spilling from an uncorked barrel, and was replaced by an overwhelming sadness and a sense of disorientation and disembodiment from the world. He wanted to cry, and tried to, but the tears would not come. Of all the questions crowding his mind, there was only one that seemed to matter now, "What have you done to Satomi?"

"What do you see?" the woman cried out again, ignoring Taylor's question. "When you look at me, what do you see?"

Taylor shook his head. "A murderer!"

"Am I a Hedalt?"

Taylor laughed scornfully; the absurdity of what was happening had reached a new level, "What are you talking about? Of course not!"

"Then what – or who – do you see?" Each word was stressed and the sentence took on an intensity and gravity that made Taylor take it more seriously than the first time she had asked. He rose to his feet and the woman threatened him again with the weapon, but Taylor was careful not to provoke her further.

"I see a woman, of course. What sort of stupid question is that?" He pointed to the body on the deck, without taking his eyes off the unnamed Commander. "What did you do to Satomi? If she's dead, I swear, you'll be next!"

"Captain, why are you talking to it?" yelled Casey, her voice shaking. Taylor had forgotten she was still there. "Why are you calling it a woman? Kill it!"

"Casey, go check on Satomi, help her if you can!" Taylor called back, but Casey did not move to help Satomi; she was still rooted to the spot, as if she'd seen a ghost. Taylor peered over at her, seeing her clearly for the first time since his fall from the containers, and like Satomi, she appeared strange as if her skin had been painted. The woman's voice drew his attention back to her, before he could study Casey further.

"Listen very carefully," said the woman in a diplomatic but serious tone. "What I'm going to say will sound insane, but once I've said it, look around you, and look at your crew mates – really look – and you'll know I'm telling you the truth."

"I'm not listening to anything until Satomi gets medical help!" Taylor growled.

"You can't help her!" the woman hit back. "That's not Satomi Rose, any more than you are the real Captain Taylor Ray, or that other simulant over there is your pilot, Casey Valera."

This got Taylor's attention, "How the hell do you know our names?"

"If you can see me as a human female then something about you is unique," the woman went on, ignoring his question again. "Some part of you is actually the man you believe you are, but how that's possible, I don't know, and I need to find out."

"I... don't understand..."

"There's too much to explain now," said the woman, "And I'm not sure you're even capable of understanding; but I'll give you the cold hard facts, and then we'll see."

"Captain..." Casey said, her voice was

breaking, and sounded even stranger because of it. Taylor turned back to face her, studying her features more closely, conscious of what the woman had said, and though her expression and body and even her hair were an exact likeness for Casey Valera, it was not her. It was like he was looking at an intricately detailed model of Casey; a mannequin come to life.

He looked down at his own hands and they were the same, and then he felt his face, and where there should have been thick stubble, there was only the smooth feeling of something soft, but also artificial. There was sensation; he could feel his fingers touching his face, but what he was feeling was not skin.

"What's happened to me?!" Taylor shouted to the woman, stumbling back and dropping to both knees. "What's happened to my body?!"

Casey could stand it no longer; she ran to and dropped down beside Satomi's corpse, which she saw as real, and bloodied from her wounds, and then saw Satomi's weapon lying at her side. She peered back across to Taylor, seeing him also as human and real, and then her eyes moved over to what she still saw as a Hedalt soldier, fixated on Taylor. She slumped down over her friend, burying her face into Satomi's chest, pretending to cry, but at the same time, she slid her hand slowly towards the handle of the sidearm.

"The Hedalt did this to you, Taylor," the woman began, oblivious to Casey's actions. "I am an officer in Earth Fleet, the same as you; the real you that lived and died centuries ago." She then gestured to the hangar bay with her free hand, while keeping the weapon aimed at Taylor's chest. "Look around you, Captain; this is an Earth Fleet base. You can see the Nimrods now, can't you?" Taylor glanced again at the rows of ships that he had first seen as Hedalt Corvettes, but were now clearly Earth Fleet vessels, as the woman had said, but he did not respond to the question. "Earth Fleet Command built this base in secret before we finally lost the war, and ensured it remained hidden from the Hedalt Empire."

"Lost the war? We won!"

The woman shook her head and lowered the weapon fractionally, aiming it just off to his side, "No, Captain, Earth lost."

Taylor shook his head, angrily, "That's a lie! I've spent the last four years searching the galaxy for the remains of the Hedalt Empire. We beat them; we destroyed their world and scattered them across the stars! Earth was saved!"

"The Hedalt have altered your memories, or the memories of the original Captain Taylor Ray, in any case," The woman continued, sounding assured. "It was Earth that was nuked, Captain, not the Hedalt home world. A not so subtle distinction, but as it turned out an easy one for them to cheat your mind into believing. We're an arrogant race; of course you'd believe we won!"

"You can't make me believe that," Taylor yelled at her. "It's madness!"

"Look at your body, Captain. Look at this hangar. The truth is staring you in the face. The truth *is* you!"

"But if we lost and everyone was killed, how did you survive? What are you doing out here, thousands of light years from Earth?"

The woman stepped closer to Taylor, lowering the weapon to her side, "We knew the war was lost at least two years before our defenses finally fell," the woman answered, suddenly sounding melancholy and, ironically, more human, "but we couldn't let that be known publicly; we had to fight on, to try to win even if we knew it was impossible. The Hedalt were not interested in surrender; for them, only our total annihilation would mean victory. So, Earth Fleet Command instigated an emergency protocol to preserve the species, and perhaps one day give us a shot at fighting back, so we could reclaim what had been taken from us. It was called the Contingency. That's where you are now, Captain. This is almost all that remains of human civilization." Then she laughed. "Actually, it seems that I'm all that remains of it."

"No, you're lying!" Taylor yelled and again he lunged at the woman, but though she had lowered her weapon, she had not lowered her guard, and she dodged the attack and struck him again. The dull thud of the weapon against his head knocked him flat on his chest, but though he physically had the strength to stand, he had lost the will to do so. He rolled onto his back and then sat up burying his face into his knees. "This is lunacy. Why are you saying this? Who the hell are you, anyway?"

"My name is Commander Sarah Sonner," the woman said, "and you are a twisted invention of Hedalt science; a corruption of technology and biology, engineered to do the Hedalt's dirty work, and hunt down what remains of humanity to extinction."

"No!" Casey cried out, leaping to her feet and firing at the figure that she still saw as a Hedalt soldier, but her entire body was shaking and the shots flew wild and wide.

Taylor's head snapped towards Casey as the crack of the weapon rang out in the hangar. He twisted back to the woman who claimed to be Commander Sarah Sonner and saw her angle her own weapon towards Casey. Taylor reached out to Commander Sonner, shouting for her to stop, but his vision flickered and faded, like a faulty computer terminal, and then he felt his body go limp. Crashing to the cold metal deck his eyes darkened and he heard more gunshots ring out, before everything fell silent and still. He had once again entered the void, only this time he felt and thought nothing at all, and simply hung in deep space, unable to move, suspended in front of a door that shone like starlight.

FIFTEEN

Taylor didn't know for how long he had remained suspended in front of the starlight door, which had continued to stay closed. Time seemed to have a different rhythm in this place, wherever and whatever it was. At first he had been afraid, partly because he was recalling the trauma of the events that had just transpired, but something about the tranquility of his ethereal location helped him to wrestle those emotions into a box, at least temporarily. Yet he couldn't stop thinking of Satomi and Casey, and how their faces and bodies had appeared so unreal, in the same way that his own body had felt unnatural after waking from the fall. Simulants, Commander Sonner had called them. He didn't yet know what that meant, but he was no longer as horrified by the knowledge of what he might be as he had been in the hangar. Perhaps there was also something meditative and even rehabilitative about this other-worldly location; something that allowed his mind to process and accept a radical new reality. Whatever the reason was, he was grateful for it.

He watched the starlight door, pondering what could be on the other side, and as he did so it began to fade to darkness, as it had done previously. Once again, Taylor felt a sensation of falling, without actually falling. Then came total darkness and a numb silence, before sensation began to return to his limbs and extremities. At the same time the physical manifestations of the emotions that had tormented his body withdrew and eventually vanished. He could still feel fear and anger and joy and everything in-between, but his body was cut off from the effects. The gut-wrenching tug of fear; the tingle of excitement; the blood-pumping rush of anger – all were gone. All were contained only in his mind.

Taylor opened his eyes. For a moment he just saw a multicolored fuzz of light and then slowly the image resolved and he saw Commander Sarah Sonner sitting in a tarnished-looking office chair in front of him. He appeared to be restrained in a similar chair, though he did not recognize the location where he was being held. But from the layout and spartan décor, he guessed that it was perhaps an office or meeting space, just off from the main hangar.

"I'm sorry about the restraints," said Sonner, sounding sincere, "but until I can be sure of what you are, and if I can trust you, I'm afraid they are necessary. I'd suggest you don't struggle, or they will only tighten further."

Taylor didn't care about the restraints; he wasn't concerned for himself. "Where are Satomi and Casey?" he demanded.

"How do you feel?" queried Sonner, yet again ignoring his question, but then added with genuine curiosity, "if you can actually feel, that is?"

"What have you done with Casey and Satomi?" Taylor asked again, more forcefully, but without overt aggression. He realized he was in no position to make demands, but despite the upsetting revelations about himself and his crew, the question of their fates weighed heavy on his mind, and he had to know.

Sonner gestured to Taylor's left, "Why don't you take a look for yourself?"

Taylor scowled and then turned his head to see Casey and Satomi propped upright in chairs four or five meters away, just outside of his peripheral vision. The sudden and intense shock of seeing their mannequin-like shells caused him to curse out loud; something he rarely did. He forced himself to keep looking, noting their synthetic skin was a grayish flesh color that shone under the harsh strip lights with a luster like silk. Their facial features were unmistakably those of Satomi and Casey, and at a glance they could easily be mistaken for humans, but observed from this distance the artificiality of their construction was plain to see. His eyes lingered on what was Satomi Rose, and a deep sadness and grief overcame him, though his body remained immune to the sensation.

"How can I be sure this isn't some trick?" asked Taylor, still shaken and still fighting against accepting what he was confronted with, despite it literally staring him in the face. "You could have drugged me while I was unconscious on the hangar deck. This could all just be an elaborate Hedalt ruse to get me to reveal some classified information," he added, defiantly. He was actually starting to convince himself of that possibility; it certainly made more sense than anything Sonner had told him. "Well, it won't work!"

Sonner rubbed her eyes and face and slumped forward, suddenly looking exhausted and pale, like she was suffering from a really bad hangover. She sniffed and rubbed her nose and then reached over to a screen set off to her side, which was covered with a simple white sheet and set on castors. She stood up, an act that seemed to require immense effort, and slowly wheeled it in front of Taylor. Despite the screen looking new, the castors squeaked as if they were ancient museum pieces. Taylor realized this was probably close to the truth, given the age of the base. He stared at the screen and then at Sonner.

"What's this?"

Sonner didn't answer and instead drew back the sheet covering the screen to reveal a mirror. Taylor peered at the silvery surface and was struck dumb. Staring back at him was his face, but it was covered with the same mannequin-like, silky, gray skin that he'd seen on Satomi and Casey. He moved the muscles – if that was even what they were – in his mouth and cheeks, and his face reacted, but with a plasticine tautness that was quite unlike the memory of his own slightly golden skin, which had become lined with age during their four-year mission. More unsettling were his eyes; instead of piercing blue irises, which glistened with life, he saw shining silvery metal orbs peering back at him. He moved and the reflection moved, and the silver orbs tracked him precisely.

He should have been nauseated by the mannequin staring back at him, but his body produced no physical response; there was no tightening of the gut or thumping of his heart or trembling hands. Everything he felt was locked inside his head, but even this was traumatic enough to make Taylor want to close his eyes and shut out what he'd seen.

"That's enough..." said Taylor, looking away from the mirror, but the image of his reflection was still clear in his mind's eye.

"This is who you are, Captain Taylor Ray," said Sonner, "I know it must be a hell of a shock, and I have no idea how I would process it if our places were reversed, but this is actually good news!"

Taylor laughed, and though it was unmistakably his laugh, it sounded strange to his ears. "How can this possibly be good news? If you're right then Earth was nuked and I'm some kind of freakish android puppet of the Hedalt Empire. There's nothing about that that's good!"

"You are alive, Captain," replied Sonner, speaking the words as if they bore great significance. "For the first time since you were created, you are truly aware of who and what you are. You're no longer a puppet, can't you see that? You're unique."

"Take it away, damn you!" he cried, this time angrily, keeping his silver eyes tight shut. He didn't want to hear that this thing that had happened to him was some kind of miraculous awakening that he should somehow be grateful for. The rage inside him should have set his blood pressure soaring, but other than the pressure of the seat and the sensation of the thick metal binds that held him, there was no physical response. Yet the emotions were real; terror, surprise, disgust, anger and contempt, he recognized them all, and felt them all at once inside his mind.

Sonner pushed the mirror to the side; the castors squeaking as it moved away. "It's gone, you can open your eyes again."

Taylor did so, but was careful only to look at Sonner and not at the mannequins to his left.

"Look, Captain, the deal is this; everything about the existence you remember is a lie," Sonner began, squeezing her own eyes tightly and wearily rubbing her face and nose. "The life you believe you have lived did not belong to you. You have a version of Taylor Ray's memories, of his home and friends and his life on Earth, but you experienced none of it. I have no idea how long you've been active for, but for all of that time, however long it was, your existence has just been an intricate fabrication. A sort of dream world blended with the real world."

The mention of a dream world made him think of the void he'd experienced, but he was not yet ready to confide anything to this woman. For all he knew, this could still be a trick, but it was becoming increasingly harder to convince himself of that. All he could do was try to find out more information; to see if his questions could reveal a chink in Sonner's story, or if they merely added to the weight of evidence that he was what she claimed him to be.

"So if I'm not the real Taylor Ray, who or what am I?" Taylor asked her.

"A simulant," said Sonner, in a purely matter-of-fact manner. "Your body is entirely artificial, as I'm sure you now realize, but your brain is the real deal. It's the only part of you that's organic."

"Organic? You mean I have a human brain?"

"Yes, it's a lab-grown replica of the brain that originally belonged to Captain Taylor Ray," said Sonner and then she coughed weakly and sniffed again. "Captain Ray's ship and crew were captured at the beginning of the war. In fact, it may have even been the very first engagement of the entire conflict."

This latest revelation should have appalled Taylor even more than the others, but the fact that his brain was real actually made him feel slightly better. Whether his brain was born and nurtured or lab-grown did not seem to matter; it made him more than merely a collection of polymers, metals and whatever else went into the construction of a simulant. Sonner seemed to be waiting for Taylor to respond, but since she received only a contemplative silence, she decided to continue.

"We, as in Earth Fleet Command, first became aware of the Hedalt Empire's experimentations with simulants towards the end of the war,"

Sonner went on, "but we only learned the full extent of their plans after Earth was destroyed, and the Contingency was set in motion."

"But why do I remember things so differently?" asked Taylor. Then he realized he hadn't phrased the question correctly. He wasn't even sure how to phrase it. "I don't just mean events, but everything else too."

Sonner's eyes narrowed and she appeared confused, or in pain, or possibly both. Either way, Taylor tried to clarify what he meant. "Why did I see you before as a Hedalt soldier, and now as... you? Why did I see rows of Hedalt Corvettes in the hangar, and now I see Nimrods? Why did I see myself as human? Why do I remember Earth surviving if it was after I was..." he paused, searching for the right word, and then added, awkwardly, "made or built or whatever the hell they did to create me."

Sonner let out a rasping cough and massaged her chest, "It's complicated, but I'll tell you what I know," she said, standing up and flexing her arms and legs. "But bear with me, because the background context is important."

"I'm apparently not going anywhere," said Taylor, surprising Sonner and even himself at his ability to joke under the circumstances.

"I don't know how much of this will marry up with what your lab-grown brain remembers, but here goes…" Sonner began, gently exercising her neck, which looked stiff and tense. "The Hedalt race have a physiological hypersensitivity to space travel. It's why they originally came 'in peace', as the cliché goes. They needed the pretense of friendship to give them time to build up an armada and get it close to the solar system through their network of jump nodes."

"You mean the Fabric?" said Taylor, feeling the need to clarify and question everything Sonner was saying, to make sure what he knew matched up with reality. Or at least the version of reality that Sonner was presenting to him, which could have still been a lie, for all he knew.

"Yes, though we only became aware of the Fabric and what the Hedalt called the CoreNet after their ill-fated arrival," Sonner replied. "Hell, we didn't even have jump tech at that time. We had to figure it out from a captured Hedalt ship, after the fighting started." Then she added, wistfully. "That was part of my job, actually."

"So what does this have to do with why my memories were altered?" Taylor cut-in, conscious that Sonner was wavering off track in her clearly debilitated state.

The Earth Fleet Commander scowled back at him, "I said, bear with me, didn't I?" she replied, snarkily, "Are all simulants so damn impatient?"

"I wouldn't know, because you shot the only

169

other examples..." Taylor hit back, with matching tenacity.

Sonner seemed oddly impressed by Taylor's pluck, but didn't react and instead picked up where she had left off earlier.

"At first, we didn't understand why the Hedalt had attacked; it wasn't like they had a shortage of other worlds they could colonize," Sonner continued, "But once we managed to gather some intelligence, their motives became clearer." Sonner flicked out her index finger. "Firstly, they specifically wanted Earth. We don't know why, but they saw it as some kind of damn trophy to hang on their wall." Sonner then flicked out her middle finger. "Secondly, they needed Humans. Or, to be more specific, they needed our human brains."

Taylor frowned. Even without the ability to feel physical revulsion, the notion of an alien species attacking Earth because they wanted to harvest human brains was deeply disquieting.

"I'm know I'm going to regret asking this," he said, knowing what was inside his own artificial head, "but why did they specifically need human brains?..."

SIXTEEN

Sonner smiled weakly and then coughed again. She was obviously struggling, but managed to soldier on, regardless. "Their need for human brains is where you fit in," she answered, pointing a finger at Taylor. "But, I'm sure you've guessed that part already."

"Something about the lab-grown human brain you mentioned me having sort of gave it away..." Taylor replied, sarcastically.

Sonner croaked a laugh, and then nodded. "Remember me saying that space travel was dangerous – even fatal – to most Hedalt? That's why they created these simulant automatons; they needed bodies to drive the expansion of their empire. But they wanted them to be adaptable, self-sufficient and subservient, and they needed a sophisticated machine for that to work. An organic computer, if you like."

"So, you're saying they, what... programmed my brain instead of a computer?"

"Yes, in essence," said Sonner, who had moved behind her chair and was leaning on it, looking ready to collapse.

"But why not just program a computerized brain," said Taylor, "you know, an AI? Surely that would be a lot easier?"

Sonner snorted, "And you're an expert in artificial intelligence, I suppose?"

Taylor scowled, "Well, no..."

"That much is obvious..." Sonner cut back in, with extra snark, causing Taylor's scowl to deepen. "You can't just create life on a computer, Captain. None of the genius science boffins on Earth even got close to a true AI, and it seems the Hedalt couldn't do it either. But by modifying a living, sentient brain, one with its core faculties intact, they achieved something similar."

"But why?" Taylor said, starting to get frustrated both with Sonner's prickly nature and the lack of real answers. "Why did they send me out into the galaxy with this whole mixed up, made up history in my head?"

"You're no ordinary simulant, Captain Ray," Sonner answered, sounding freer and more natural than before. "After the Hedalt finally smashed through our defenses and nuked Earth, what remained of Earth Fleet fled, jumping randomly all across the galaxy, trying to escape. The Hedalt made you, and other ships and crews exactly like yours, to hunt us down."

The mention of crews compelled Taylor to chance another glance at Satomi and Casey. He managed to maintain eye contact with their immobile, lifeless frames for a few seconds, before unease compelled him to look away. The faces and bodies were manufactured, but inside the engineered skulls were real brains, the same as inside his own head. They had not been aware of what they were, not in the way he was now, but something organic had still died inside them. They were more than just machines, at least to him.

Sonner caught him glancing at them, and sensed his obvious discomfort. She felt a stab of guilt, realizing that her macabre display was in poor taste, and perhaps even cruel. She hadn't considered that a simulant could experience emotions in the same way as a human, but she couldn't afford to feel sympathy for this facsimile of Taylor Ray just yet. She still had larger concerns, one of which was ensuring this unique simulant was truly free from the Hedalt programming that had compelled him to attack her earlier.

"Before, you saw these two simulants as the

real Satomi Rose and Casey Valera," Sonner went on, continuing to lay it on the line for Taylor. "The modifications to your brain made you perceive them as human, just as they made you see me as a Hedalt soldier, an enemy you were already preconditioned to hate. The Hedalt weren't physically capable of jumping all across the galaxy hunting down Earth's survivors, so they messed with your memories and your perceptions, and programmed you to do it for them."

Taylor nodded; as crazy as it sounded, it was actually starting to make sense. "They made us believe we were hunting down the remnants of our deadly alien enemy, when in reality we were mopping up the last dregs of humanity."

Sonner laughed and then coughed bitterly, "It's hard to keep it all straight, isn't it?" Then her expression hardened and she was momentarily lost in her own thoughts. "You know, if Earth had won the war, we'd have pursued the Hedalt to the ends of the galaxy too, exactly as you thought you were doing. That's why your brain is accepting of the lie, Captain, because it's so believable. We'd have shown them no mercy, so I guess we should have expected no less in return."

Taylor thought about this for a moment. He'd always told himself that the DSR missions were about self-preservation; a necessary evil to ensure the Hedalt scourge was gone for good. Or perhaps that's just how he'd been programmed to think of them, it was impossible to know. Sonner yawned loudly and stretched, which drew his silver eyes back to her.

"Perhaps this is just some sort of cosmic karma for the brutality of Earth's history, you know?" said Sonner. "Maybe it's the universe teaching us a lesson."

"I wouldn't have put you down as someone who believed in karma or destiny," said Taylor, surprised by Sonner's comment.

Sonner shrugged. "When Earth was lost, I found it easier to believe that there had to be a reason why some of us survived, and managed to escape, unseen, to this backwater part of the galaxy. I told myself that it somehow meant the Contingency wasn't doomed to failure from the outset."

Taylor laughed and shook his head, "The universe just isn't that connected, Commander. Things happen because of what people do, whether they are humans or Hedalt, not because of any higher plan."

Sonner moved around the chair and sank heavily down into it, "I'm not talking about God or gods or anything like that."

"Then what?"

"Oh, I don't know," she said, shrugging wearily. "You have to believe in something, though, right? Look at us, for example."

Taylor laughed again; it was a strange sound that he was still getting used to. "Are you saying the two of us are entwined in some cosmic plan?"

Sonner's eyes widened, "A cynic, eh?" she said, with a hint of sass. "Look at the evidence, Captain. I alone survive here, and no sooner do I wake up, but you manage to find an unfindable base, and are somehow 'woken up' too." Sonner smiled, "Hell, you could even say that you were re-born. Why... how... I don't know, but it's one hell of a coincidence, don't you think?"

Now it was Taylor who shrugged, "Life is just a series of coincidences on a universal scale."

Sonner coughed another laugh, "See... cynic."

"What would you call it then?"

Sonner pondered the question for a few moments and then smiled again, causing her striking, strong features and sharp eyes to momentarily soften. "How about hope?"

Taylor glanced briefly at the simulant frame of Satomi and then sighed. It was an involuntary reaction – an instinctive human response prompted by a human brain – and it puzzled him that his body still reacted to emotions, even though it no longer felt them physically.

"Hope is something I can get behind," he replied, solemnly. "Most of all, I hope that this is just some insane coma-induced nightmare. I hope that any moment now I'm going to wake up and see Satomi and Casey and Blake again."

"Ah, but you already *have* woken up," said Sonner, enthusiastically. "Now you see the truth, in all its ugliness. Frankly, I'm astonished you're able to cope with any of this, what with those circuits in your head popping. I have never seen a simulant woken like you, and I've never heard of it happening before."

Sonner coughed again and then rubbed her chest to relieve the spasms, before wilting against the backrest of the chair to recover her breath. That her condition seemed to be worsening hadn't gone unnoticed by Taylor, and he found himself worrying about her; another involuntary human response.

"No offence, but you look terrible."

Sonner managed another croaky laugh, "Gee, thanks."

"Are you sick?"

Sonner shook her head, but then changed her mind and half-shrugged a confirmation. "Sort of. It's stasis sickness; I was stuck inside that damned chamber for a hell of a lot longer than I was supposed to be."

"How much longer?" Taylor remembered that Satomi had not been able to accurately assess for how long the stasis chambers had been active.

"Oh, about two hundred and seventy-five

years longer, according to the time recorder on the base," said Sonner, speaking the number as dismissively as if she was apologizing for being a couple of minutes late to a meeting. "We were supposed to be in stasis for fifty years," she went on, "enough time for this base to automate the manufacturing of our new Nimrod Fleet, and long enough that the Hedalt would have assumed the human plague to have been cleansed from the galaxy, giving us the element of surprise." Then she looked Taylor in his silvery eyes and sighed, "Sadly, it would seem that we vastly under-estimated quite how persistent those alien bastards would be, seeing as they're still hunting us three hundred and twenty-five years later."

"Did you know the others, in the stasis chambers, I mean?" asked Taylor, suddenly realizing that Sonner must also be dealing with an enormous emotional burden. She was not only coping with the loss of Earth, but also of the loss of one hundred and fifty-nine of the last remnants of humanity, many of whom she must have known personally. He could see from Sonner's reaction that it was a distressing subject, but Taylor was still keen to move their discussion away from himself, because it meant respite from having to face the fantastical new reality that Sonner was describing to him. The less he thought about what he was, the more at ease he felt, and the more he felt like himself. *Myself? Am I even really Taylor Ray?*

"Yes, I knew many of them; most were colleagues, but some of them were my friends too. One or two I knew closely..." Sonner's reply seemed to drift off and she suddenly looked desolate as well as exhausted. It only lasted a moment, before she composed herself and continued, "This base was built in a hurry and I guess some jackass didn't do their job right." Then she smiled and held up her hands, "But, hey, I'm still here. One Earth Fleet officer against the entire horde!".

The mention of numbers reminded Taylor that Sonner had said there were more ships and crews like his. He stole another glance at Satomi and Casey, pondering what that could mean. "How many are there?" he asked, his head hung low. "Simulants like me, I mean."

"In total? Millions. Billions. The honest answer is I don't know," said Sonner, shrugging. Then she raised a quivering finger at Satomi, "But if your question is how many are there of you four, as in Captain Taylor Ray, Satomi Rose and the rest of your crew... Well, that's a different question, though no less tricky to answer."

"Why?" asked Taylor leaning forward in the chair, as much as possible given the restraints, which he'd almost forgotten about until that point, since he felt no discomfort or pain.

"Our intel told us the Hedalt had successfully harvested ten brains in total," explained Sonner, "You see, brain harvesting was the hardest part. It required months to extract all of the memories and other synaptic nuances that made that person who they were."

"You mean, their soul?" said Taylor, trying to condense what Sonner was saying into a simpler concept.

"I thought you were too cynical to believe in such things?" replied Sonner, recalling the sterile way Taylor had talked about the nature of life only moments earlier.

Taylor glanced down at his feet, "I never used to believe in anything like that," he said, quietly, "but now... I don't know. I guess I need to believe that I'm something more than just a laboratory experiment."

Sonner observed Taylor's sorrowful reaction, recognizing it as a genuine and natural human emotion; something that could not be faked. *Whatever he is, there is something still human inside...* she told herself.

"There are the four brains that crewed the Hunter ships; ships like yours, Captain," Sonner continued, though Taylor was still staring blankly at his feet. "These are simulants in the truest sense; near perfect replicas, possessing the memories, experiences and personality traits of their original hosts, just altered to perceive the universe differently."

Taylor let out a pitiful laugh. "'Hunter ships'... We called it 'deep space recon'."

Sonner smiled. "More believable that way, isn't it? The honorable Earth Fleet wouldn't deliberately hunt aliens to extinction; instead they do reconnaissance to track down the remains of a belligerent and hostile nemesis..."

"What about the other six?"

"Those were used for everything else," replied Sonner, "But they were lobotomized automatons, not at all like you. They were programmed to work in factories, mines and so on, and many of them were used to crew their ships. It's how they were able to vastly expand their armada, and eventually crush us."

"You mean they're used as slaves..." said Taylor, condensing Sonner's description into the cold, simple truth.

"Yes," said Sonner, though she was loath to admit it. She preferred to avoid using this description because the thought of millions of human-cybernetic slaves made her blood boil. As if the Hedalt nearly succeeding in committing speciocide wasn't already bad enough, the fact they had enslaved human brains to do their work was almost worse than annihilation. "As I said, there could be millions, even billions of those by now, but after three hundred and twenty-five years, it's quite possible you could be the last Hunter in the galaxy." Then Sonner held up her hands, "Sorry, deep space recon ship."

Taylor was silent for a time, trying to process everything that Sonner had said. The evidence backed up her story, but then how could he trust what he was seeing or hearing? If Sonner was correct, he'd spent his entire life living a lie. It was impossible even to know how long had he been alive, if 'alive' was the right way to describe his existence.

As he was pondering these questions, Sonner got up and moved behind him. Taylor frowned, his artificial face reproducing the expression faithfully, but then a moment later the binders restraining his arms and legs fell loose. He brought his hands around to the front and stared at them; they didn't ache, as he would have expected them to after so long held in restraints. He flexed his fingers and watched the pale pink-gray digits move as instinctively as real hands. He was suddenly aware of Sonner watching him with interest, and he stood up, grabbing the back of the chair for support, which crumpled under his grip. He stared at the mangled metal in astonishment.

"You'll have to get used to your new strength," said Sonner, "Honestly, these binders would never have contained you if you had tried to break free, not that you knew that, of course."

Taylor let go of the chair and held his hands in front of him, away from his body, as if they were explosive charges that could go off at any moment.

"Why have you released me?"

"When I fought you, and attacked your crew, it was because you were my enemy; just a simulant doing the will of the Hedalt."

Taylor again glanced to the two bodies at the side, and the pain of losing them surged inside his mind like a reflex. He forced himself to look away and back into Sonner's tired eyes. "And now?"

Sonner folded her arms and peered intently back into Taylor's silver orbs, which despite being made of metal, still somehow glinted with the spark of life. "When I came out of hibernation, I discovered I was the only one who survived; one human being out of the one hundred and sixty that made it out here. But now, we are two. And if I'm going to take the fight back to the Hedalt and kick their alien asses out of Earth, I'm going to need everyone I can get, including you, Captain Ray. Because, for reasons I can't fathom, and against my better judgement, I truly believe that's who you really are."

Sonner's heartfelt answer came as a surprise to Taylor, and he felt lifted by it. "Well, that makes one of us, at least, but I appreciate your trust." Despite being unsure of what he was, he still felt like an officer in Earth Fleet, and knowing what he now did about the true fate of Earth, he found himself feeling as Sonner did; a compulsion to do his duty, and fight back.

"Give it time, Captain," Sonner continued, "time to get to know yourself, and the truly unique individual you are now."

Taylor nodded then held out his hand. Sonner hesitated, looking at the mangled chair. "Don't worry, I'm not going to crush it."

Sonner took his hand and shook it. "That's my second gesture of trust. Now it's your turn, cynic."

"I'm not actually a cynic," said Taylor. "In fact, I was always the optimistic one. Always the one to see the glass half-full. Or I used to be."

"You can be again. You can be whatever you want to be, Taylor Ray, and do anything."

Taylor looked at Casey and Satomi and forced himself not to look away this time. He hated what the Hedalt had turned them into, and had turned him into. "I don't know what I am, or what I can become," he said, turning back to Sonner, "but I do know that I want to fight whoever did this to me."

SEVENTEEN

Sonner operated the recovery crane system in the hangar control room while Taylor peered out through the thick window that overlooked the landing deck outside. He was lost in his own thoughts, trying to process everything he'd been told and everything he'd experienced since waking up from the Hedalt programming. He and his crew had entered the lava tube expecting to find yet another ghost base, but the only ghost he had discovered was the pale reflection that had stared back at him in the mirror. It was the face of a man who had lived and died over three centuries earlier. *So what the hell does that make me now?* Taylor wondered.

He considered that everything he had ever

believed in was a lie, fabricated by the Hedalt to induce him into doing their dirty work. But they hadn't invented everything, Taylor told himself. His brain was still human, which meant that his emotions and feelings were real, as were those of his crew. In amongst the lies there must also have been truth, he asserted – and he had to find it before he could truly understand who he was.

Suddenly the exterior of the base was bathed in a bright white light, which startled Taylor out of his daydreaming. He glanced across to see that Sonner had turned on the external floodlights and was maneuvering the powerful cranes towards Taylor's ship with the intention of bringing it inside the hangar for repair. The ship stood on the same landing pad, precisely where Casey had so skillfully landed it, but the vessel he was staring at was no longer a Nimrod-class cruiser, but a Hedalt Corvette-class cruiser. It was another of the many unbelievable changes that his now conscious mind had to accept, and as he watched the ship begin to slide into the giant hangar airlock, he wondered if it would still feel like the home he'd known for close to four years. *Has it even really been four years?* he wondered. He could take nothing for granted now.

How long he'd been in space was just another one of the many questions that dominated his thoughts, most of which terrified him, but of all the questions he sought answers to, the one that preoccupied his mind the most was what to do next. In a remarkable leap of faith, Sonner had chosen to trust him and to treat him as another human – despite the only biological element of his body being the brain inside his simulant skull. But although he felt human, he no longer knew what being human meant.

Sonner had given Taylor a datapad, with access to records of the Earth-Hedalt war, and he'd spent some time anxiously skimming through its contents while the Commander worked to recover his ship. There was far too much information to assimilate, but he had managed to gain a condensed history of the conflict, and it made for harrowing reading. Earth as he remembered it was no more. Based on the final scans of the planet by the Earth Fleet ships that had fled to the Contingency base, every major city and built-up area had been annihilated. The Hedalt had been merciless, levelling the planet to such a degree that it was almost like sending it back to primordial times.

He thought about the apartment he'd intended to buy in Astoria and how he recalled being there in one of the strange visions he'd had after falling; visions he'd still not discussed with Sonner. *Had I already owned the apartment?* Taylor mused. *Or were the Hedalt just using an earlier memory, before it was mine? A way to give me something to look forward to, and strive towards?* He didn't know and perhaps would never know, not that any of it mattered, because everything that the original Taylor Ray had known was gone. He found it curious that he still possessed the jumbled mash-up of the real Taylor's memories combined with the memories of his 'life' with Satomi, Casey and Blake, but they all seemed superfluous in light of Sonner's disclosures. For all intents and purposes he had died on the floor of the hangar deck, and this was the first day of his actual life. His will to survive was strong, as strong as any real human's, and his need to do something positive was undiminished; he just didn't know what.

The airlock cycle completed and Sonner switched to the hangar's internal cranes in order to set the damaged Hedalt Corvette down in the primary maintenance bay, where a small army of worker bots and drones set to the task of repairing it. He watched the automated robots for a time, noting that the damage to ship was clearly as a result of conventional Earth Fleet ordnance, rather than Hedalt plasma weapons, which his datapad had mentioned only came into use later in the war. The Corvette-class cruisers had pre-dated such technology; in effect, his ship was no more advanced than the Earth Fleet Nimrods, which made it three centuries out-of-date compared to whatever the Hedalt Empire had in their armada now. How they were going to succeed with just the two of them and one ancient ship was a question he didn't want to think about at that moment.

He tried to distract himself from this and the other bigger questions by focusing on the immediate ones, and strolled up beside Sonner, who acknowledged his arrival with a warm smile.

"I don't know why you're making such an effort to recover that alien monstrosity," said Taylor, peering down at the angular black ship, which lacked the elegant lines and curves of the Nimrod. "Why not just take out one of these brand-new Nimrod-class cruisers?"

Sonner shut off the controls and turned to face him, resting back against the console. She still looked exhausted and on the verge of collapse. "We'd attract way too much attention in a Nimrod; the Hedalt believed they destroyed our entire fleet, remember?"

Taylor hadn't considered that, but after three hundred and twenty-five years, the appearance of an Earth Fleet ship would cause something of a stir. "Fair point; I guess that if we did pleasure-cruise around the galaxy in a Nimrod, it would sort of give the game away."

"That would be an understatement," Sonner answered, smiling at him, "and we need to stay hidden for as long as possible."

"Well, at least with it inside the hangar it means I don't need to recover my environment suit," said Taylor. But then he had a realization; he tapped his synthetic chest and added, "though I guess I don't really need to worry about toxic atmospheres anymore."

"Your brain is still human and organic," said Sonner, mimicking his gesture by tapping a finger to the side of her head. "Your body may be synthetic, but your brain still needs oxygen. So those environment suits weren't only there to maintain the illusion."

Taylor nodded, appreciating that it was going to take some time to get used to his new reality. In many ways his body was tougher than an old tractor, but he was far from indestructible. Blake, Casey and Satomi were evidence enough that he was just as mortal as any human.

"Do you even know how to fly a Hedalt ship?" asked Taylor, turning from the morbid and upsetting thoughts of death and his crew to the practicalities of what they should do next.

"No, but that's not your run-of-the-mill Hedalt Corvette," Sonner answered, after a long breathy yawn. "Inside, the main bridge and some other sections are configured to look the same as a Nimrod," Sonner continued, while stepping down the metal staircase to the main deck and inviting Taylor to follow. "It's all part of the ruse. They can trick your mind into seeing and feeling things that are not real, but in many cases simply changing the environment to match what your brain expects to see is easier than changing your brain's perception of it. Besides, from what little we did learn about the Hunter ships, we got the impression that it was important to include real objects too. Maybe it helped to maintain the fiction somehow."

Taylor nodded; re-engineering the ship would be a lot simpler than re-engineering a brain, he assumed. But this made him wonder what else the Hedalt had made him perceive differently.

"Before I was... woken, or whatever you call this, I saw you as a..." he hesitated, trying to find the right word, and settled on the crudest and most obvious one, "a monster. Actually, a monster with a plasma rifle... Is that really what the Hedalt are, or was that a lie too?"

Sonner raised an eyebrow. "A monster? Like with three heads and a spiky tail?"

Taylor laughed, "Not quite that monstrous, but certainly frightening enough to give a child nightmares."

"I don't know how you saw me, but monsters would be a good way to describe the Hedalt, at least in terms of their actions."

"But they don't look like monsters?"

Sonner glanced sideways at him, but continued walking, "No, not at all. They don't actually look all that different to us, really. Two legs, two arms, one head... no spiky tail."

Taylor laughed again, "I think you read too many stories about dragons or demons as a girl."

"They were fairy tales compared to the reality, I'm afraid," said Sonner, darkly. "They do have plasma weapons, though. They were introduced later in the war, along with the newer, more powerful ships of their expanded, simulant-crewed armada. It was at that point we realized we had no hope of winning."

"But I saw you shooting plasma shards at us," said Taylor, still struggling to get his new simulant head around the complexities.

"I wish I had a plasma rifle, but sadly not," replied Sonner. "Just another deception. If you check out the damage to the base now, you'll see bullet holes and marks from ricochets, not plasma burns and scorches. Though the explosive-tipped rounds did make a bit of a mess."

Taylor shook his head, "It's hard to believe they look like us, though. I mean you. Humans, I mean," babbled Taylor, until he got the right words out. "The chances of that are..." he threw up his hands, unable to put a number on the impossibly small odds.

"The science boffins at Earth Fleet Command said that their remarkably humanoid appearance was an 'implausible coincidence'."

"It sounds like those science boffins had a talent for understatement."

Sonner laughed, but it was a tired, drowsy laugh done out of politeness.

"I suppose it's easier to hunt and kill monsters than people that look like you," said Taylor, who was beginning to understand the intricacies of the deception that the Hedalt had created.

"People are easier to manipulate than you'd think," Sonner answered, "At first, they 'came in peace'; it was all very sci-fi and exciting. But sadly our blinkered romanticism made us foolish and careless. No-one comes in peace, Captain Taylor Ray; every living creature in the universe wants something and is willing to take it by force."

"I don't believe that."

Sonner smiled, "Well, you are only a couple of hours old; you'll learn."

Taylor laughed. Sonner wasn't wrong; everything he thought he knew about the universe he'd have to re-learn, like a child taking their first steps, but he wasn't a child, nor was he naive. The memories, skills and experiences that the Hedalt had transferred from the original Taylor Ray were alive inside him, and he could still draw from them, and build on them with the new knowledge he now had access to.

"Where do you intend to go?" asked Taylor, focusing back in on their current objective, which was to fix up the battered Corvette. "A single human, one traumatized simulant and a beat-up old Hedalt Corvette won't be much use against the combined might of an entire empire."

Sonner stopped and frowned at him. "No, it won't, but it's a start." She then gestured to the long row of Nimrod-class cruisers, with the black Hedalt cruiser parked in front of them, slightly smaller and meaner-looking in comparison, like a scorpion in the middle of a line of songbirds. "The Contingency included plans for three bases, with this as the main combat base and shipyard. We built it the furthest distance away from Earth that we could find a suitable location for. The fact that no-one from any of the other bases came here in over three hundred years means there's a chance they're still out there, still in stasis, like I was."

"Or it could mean that they're already dead..." Taylor stopped himself; he sounded more like Blake than his usual optimistic self. Thinking about his grumpy TacSpec officer reminded him of the fateful firefight on the balcony around the command center. He remembered how Blake had fallen and was crushed, and recalled how Casey had rushed to his aid and managed to lift the metal girder off his body. The reason for this mammoth feat of strength was obvious to him now, given how much strength his own simulant body possessed since its awakening, but Casey hadn't been awake, Taylor realized. *What does that mean?* Taylor asked himself. *Deep down, did her fear of losing Blake temporarily wake a part of her up?*

Sonner studied Taylor's pensive expression, "What's going on in that brain of yours?"

"Oh, nothing..." lied Taylor. He wasn't really sure what he was thinking, and he didn't want to talk to Sonner until he'd straightened things out in his own head. "At least, I'm not sure yet. I'll let you know when I figure it out."

Sonner nodded, "I can't imagine how this must feel for you; but, I'm afraid I can't give you much more time to reflect on your options, such as they are. I need to get back out there and find the others. Too much time has been lost already."

Taylor studied the Hedalt Corvette; with an entire hangar's worth of maintenance equipment focused solely on it, the repairs were progressing rapidly and were almost done.

"I wish I had more time to digest all of this," said Taylor. "This day hasn't really gone the way I imagined it would."

Sonner sighed and rubbed her face; she still felt like death warmed up as a result of her extended hibernation. "Look, Captain, things haven't turned out as expected for either of us," she began. "I don't know why I alone survived, and I don't know how you're able to understand what you are. All I know is that I'm alive and so are you, and that the Hedalt are still out there. So long as I'm still breathing, the Contingency has a chance, and that means I have a job to do."

The repair drones peeled away from the Hedalt Corvette and the hubbub of noise slowly died down. The calm that replaced it was deafening.

"Decision time, Captain, what's it to be?"

Taylor again thought about Casey's feat of strength – a blip in an otherwise unbroken fantasy – and how he had broken free of his own mental prison. And then he thought about Satomi's broken simulant body, and how it contained an organic brain. It wasn't the real Satomi Rose; from what Sonner had said, she had existed centuries earlier, like the real Taylor Ray, but to him she was real. His feelings for her were still real. And perhaps she wasn't the only Satomi Rose out there in the galaxy, and the others weren't the only Casey or Blake. Suddenly, he knew what he had to do. Fighting the Hedalt wasn't enough for him; it was an enemy he'd never truly known, and one that had destroyed a planet and a civilization that was never really his. He wanted to fight the aliens that had manipulated him and used him like a weapon, but in truth his connection to Earth was not nearly as strong as his connection to his crew, and to Satomi in particular. It had taken her to die for him to realize that, but what he also realized was that maybe there was something he could still do about it.

"I'll come with you," said Taylor, sounding resolute. "I'll help you find these other bases and, if there's any chance at all to put the Contingency into action, I'll help you to fight and destroy the Hedalt too."

Sonner nodded, but then her eyes narrowed. "So, what's the catch?"

"I need your help to find something too."

"Name it," said Sonner.

"I want to find the other simulants; the other reproductions of my crew," said Taylor, with a sudden determination. "I want to find Blake Meade, Casey Valera and Satomi Rose, and I want to wake them."

Sonner's eyes widened. "Wow, for a moment there, I was worried you were going to ask for something impossibly difficult..."

"I mean it, Commander," said Taylor, firmly. "If you consider me to be human, or at least a real person, then there's a chance I can offer the same to my crew. I owe it to them to try, and frankly, so do you." Taylor didn't want to hit her too hard, but the inference was not lost on Sonner.

"I did what I had to, Captain," Sonner hit back, and Taylor could see that he'd both offended and hurt her, "If I'd have known..."

Taylor held up a hand and bowed his head

slightly, "Hey, I'm sorry, that was unfair," he cut in. "They were trying to kill you. I was trying to kill you... It wasn't your fault."

Sonner sighed and nodded, but Taylor knew he'd opened up a wound. "They won't be the people you remember," Sonner cautioned, but there was a warmth and softness in place of her usual prickliness. "Your interactions as a crew were unique, and can't be replicated. If there are any other simulant versions of them still out there, they will know a different version of you."

"Maybe they won't be the same," Taylor replied, then he shrugged. "Maybe it can never be like it was, I don't care. All I know is I have to try."

Sonner considered Taylor's words, chewing the inside of her mouth as if she was chewing gum, and then she stretched out a hand, "It's a deal, Captain Ray."

"You can me Taylor," he said, taking Sonner's hand and shaking it, mindful of not adding too much pressure to his grip.

"Okay, Taylor," said Sonner, and then her lips curled into a wicked smile. "You can call me... Commander Sonner. We have to maintain a rank structure, after all, and I do outrank you."

Taylor laughed and found that he was actually getting used to the alien sound. Certainly every time he laughed, he felt a little more human. But after four years, or at least the memory of four years, as the ranking officer on his ship, he wasn't used to being subordinate to anyone. He thought of how Casey used to react to his orders and smiled, before lazily saluting his new superior and responding breezily with, "Aye, aye, Commander Sarah Sonner."

EIGHTEEN

Taylor stood at the door to his quarters, too afraid to step inside. Sonner had been mostly right about the internal layout of the ship being changed to match that of a Nimrod-class cruiser, but what she hadn't mentioned was just how little of it had been modified. Beyond the bridge and the four different crew quarters, along with the corridors and communal spaces that connected them, the rest of the ship was empty, dark and cold. But, as he had feared, there were also other things about these spaces that he saw differently now that the shroud had been lifted from his silver simulant eyes.

"Not quite how you remember it, I take it?" said Sonner, who was standing behind him.

"Not exactly," Taylor replied, looking at the contraption that he now saw in place of his bed. It looked more like an operating table, with conduits and wires and plugs sprouting from it like tentacles. Even more disconcerting was the compartment directly above it, which was molded in the shape of a head. He knew the question he needed to ask, but didn't want to hear the answer.

"What goes in that compartment? And please don't tell me it's my head."

"Everything about your existence up until a few hours ago was a lie," Sonner answered. "Do you really want me to lie to you now?"

Taylor shook his head, "No, I suppose not." Though in the case of the ominous head-shaped compartment, he didn't feel an urgent need to know the truth either. "What is this thing for?" he asked, gesturing to what used to be his bed.

"You didn't think that you actually spent your days literally walking around this ship, did you, like a little simulant happy family?" said Sonner snarkily, though Taylor chose to let it slide on account of her obvious exhaustion. He also become grouchy when he was tired, though he wondered if perhaps that wouldn't be a problem for him any longer. "Your simulant bodies are only needed when you embark on a planetary mission or have to physically leave the ship for another reason. For the rest of the time, you lived out your fantasy life in a sort of dream-state. In essence you existed inside each other's minds."

Taylor remembered how disorientated he had felt after waking in his cabin, before the mission had begun, and how the rest of the crew had appeared to suffer from a similar malaise. And then he recalled his strange dream-like experiences after falling from the stack of containers in the hangar, and how he had appeared in the void in space, in the corridor with the starlight door. And, before that, the memory of standing on the balcony of an apartment in Astoria, looking out across the Columbia River, and seeing Casey, Blake and Satomi there with him, but in what he now recognized as their simulant bodies. He didn't know what it all meant, but certainly what Sonner was saying made sense in a sick and twisted kind of way. The Hedalt had maintained the pretense of normal life and real human relationships, while for the most part these were just interactions between their brains, which had been neatly stored in head-shaped compartments, like some sort of gruesome nineteenth-century circus attraction.

Taylor had never hated the Hedalt, despite them having killed millions during the war, or what turned out to be his altered memory of it, in which Earth had actually prevailed. For him, serving in Earth Fleet and commanding the DSR mission was merely doing his duty. But the reality of what the Hedalt were and what they had done was far worse even than the monsters he remembered. They had destroyed the Earth of his memory and almost wiped out all human life in the galaxy – for all he knew, Sonner was the last human alive – and he had been complicit in this act of race extermination. That he had not been aware of his actions didn't matter to him; the Hedalt had manipulated him like a marionette and used him as a weapon to mop up the rest of humanity. He wondered how many missions he had really been on, and if he had ever actually destroyed a human colony. Where his memories of the four-year DSR mission were concerned, all they had ever found were ghosts, but if they had the ability to manipulate what he remembered, then perhaps they could also manipulate what he could forget.

"Can we have this thing dismantled?" asked Taylor, feeling disgusted at the sight of it. If he'd still had a stomach, he was sure it would be churning.

"I'm afraid not," said Sonner, ominously. "You'll still need to use it to maintain your simulant body."

"Taylor turned his back to the room and peered into Sonner's eyes, "You're telling me I need to plug-in and recharge?"

Sonner laughed, "No, nothing so rudimentary.

The simulant frame can harvest energy from a number of sources, including your little bed there, but remember that your brain is organic, and so it still needs to sleep."

"Great, then I'll be needing an actual bed."

"You don't need a bed..." said Sonner, nodding towards the head-shaped opening in the wall, her lips curled into a mischievous grin.

"Over my dead simulant body!" cried Taylor leaving the room and hearing the door slide shut behind him. "If I'm going to live in this frame then I'm going to live as much like a normal human being as possible. And that means I need a proper bed."

"Fair enough," said Sonner. "I can try to rig something up that interfaces with the cranial storage unit in the wall."

"Can we not talk about that?" Taylor complained, leading them towards the bridge.

"Okay..." Sonner replied, but then her lips curled into a wicked grin again, "though it does give a new meaning to needing some headspace."

Taylor stopped and spun towards her, "Look that's not funny!" he said, but was unable to stop himself from laughing, and for a few moments they were both afflicted by the giggles.

Sonner wiped a tear away from her eye, "Oh damn, I'm sorry. I really must get some sleep!"

"It's okay, laughing makes me feel... normal."

"Then I'll do my best to make you laugh as much as I can," said Sonner, warmly.

As they continued on towards the bridge, Sonner detailed the internal modifications that she planned to make to the ship so that it was more hospitable to both humans and simulants. She had already loaded a small army of the maintenance drones from the hangar into the ship's hold, since they were far superior to the Hedalt equivalent on the Corvette, and would complete the tasks with greater efficiency. Plus, if they were to suffer damage during their future adventures, the greater number of more advanced drones would be better equipped to conduct deep space repairs to the ship, too.

Taylor had pointed out that before converting the ship to be more hospitable to humans they first needed to find a few more members of Earth Fleet, but Sonner had not been deterred, and again Taylor was cross at himself for being negative. It was like he'd turned into Blake and Sonner had become him, filled with optimism even in the darkest of situations.

The door to the bridge slid open and they stepped inside. This, at least, looked completely unchanged from the way Taylor remembered it. "Finally, something that seems normal."

"Good, because you're flying," said Sonner, as she practically collapsed into the command chair.

Taylor shot her a look that, even with his artificial muscles and shimmering silver eyes, left no doubt as to his displeasure.

"Hey, I told you that we needed to maintain a rank structure, and in case you hadn't noticed, Commander outranks Captain, which makes this chair mine."

"Technically speaking, I'm a Hedalt secret operative who never enrolled in Earth Fleet," Taylor hit back, unwilling to capitulate his command so easily. "And since this is in fact a Hedalt Corvette , I believe that actually makes the chair mine."

Sonner considered this for a moment and shrugged. "That's a fair point." Then she scratched her ear and half scrunched up her face, "I'll let you into a little secret, Captain. I'm an engineering officer, so I actually don't know how to pilot this class of starship..."

Taylor laughed, not cruelly, though it was hard to tell from the way his body reproduced the sound, and the bleak expression on Sonner's face seemed to highlight this.

"No offense intended, Commander," he said, raising his hands, "It's actually nice to know that you're not infallible. It makes you... well, human."

Taylor walked over to the pilot's station and placed his hands on the back of the chair, careful not to apply too much pressure this time. This had been Casey's domain; he had never known a better natural flyer than her, or at least that's what the original Taylor's memories told him. But he'd seen her fly with his own eyes too and although not all of what he'd seen had been real, Casey's flying had to be, otherwise the ship would have been a wreck lying on the volcanic rock floor of the lava tube. The only way he would ever know for sure would be to find Casey again, somewhere out in the stars, wake her, and see if she really was the maverick pilot he remembered her to be.

He sat down in the chair and ran through the pre-flight checks, but then he noticed the flashing indicator on the main status panel, showing that the ship's connection to the CoreNet was still down, and he had a thought.

"If we leave the lava tube in this ship, it will re-establish a connection to the CoreNet," said Taylor swiveling around in the chair to face Sonner. "That would make the Hedalt suspicious and they'd want to know what happened. It might even prompt them to come out here and find out for themselves."

"Way ahead of you, Captain," said Sonner with a smug smile, "I already made sure your ship's transceiver was deactivated, while the drones were busy repairing the ship."

Taylor was impressed. "And I suppose you already deactivated the comms tower on the surface too?" Sonner's face fell, indicating that she had not.

"Is that how you found this place?" she asked, hurriedly punching a complex sequence of commands into the panel on the chair.

"Yes, though it still took some finding. In fact, if hadn't been for Satomi..." Taylor's voice trailed off abruptly as Satomi's name was spoken out loud. He looked across to her station and felt her loss keenly once again.

Sonner glanced up at Taylor, and then followed his gaze across to the mission operations console, before finishing the sequence of commands and resting forward on the chair arms.

"I'm not even sure why I'm asking, because I don't know how it would work, but was there something between you two?"

Taylor physically recoiled back into his chair and blustered a response. If his face had been capable of blushing, it would have turned a crimson red. "No, of course not. I was her commanding officer, it wouldn't have been right."

Sonner sniffed and rubbed her nose, before nodding, "Uh huh, I understand."

"I mean it! I mean, I liked her, sure, but it was purely professional," Taylor lied. He wasn't even sure why he was trying to hide it.

"Don't sweat it, Captain. They wouldn't have put you all together if there wasn't some kind of chemistry between you," said Sonner, resting back again. Then she smiled another mischievous smile. "Though it does explain why you're so eager to put the team back together. And one person in particular, I think?..."

Taylor had recovered his composure; it helped not having to deal with flutters in his stomach. "I'm keen to put the team back together, because I got them killed," he said, sourly. Then he jabbed a finger at Sonner, "and, in case you forgot, you killed them."

"And I'll help you find them again, and wake them, Captain. You have my word."

Taylor didn't yet know what this woman's word was worth, but he had no choice but to find out.

The status panel on Sonner's chair bleeped and she checked it. "The deep space comms tower has been deactivated. Let's hope that's the last malfunction this base throws at us."

"The Hedalt could still send a ship to check on what happened to us," said Taylor. "I mean, to the original us. And if they do, there's still a chance they might find this base."

Sonner rubbed her face and sighed heavily, "Yes, you're right. If they find this place then there's no hope of fighting back, no matter how many survived in the other locations. The entire Nimrod Fleet is right here."

Taylor swung his chair back around and checked his panel. Pre-flight checks had been completed and the ship was ready to launch; but they weren't the only ship in the hangar, which gave him an idea.

"What if we load the transceiver from this ship onto a Nimrod, and then crash it into one of the planets in this system?"

Sonner's face suddenly looked less fatigued. "Not a bad idea, Captain. They would conclude that it was actually this ship that had crashed on the surface."

"If they looked very closely, they might be able to see that it wasn't a Hedalt Corvette," admitted Taylor, finding fault with his own plan.

"They won't look that closely," said Sonner, confidently. "They are cold-hearted bastards who wouldn't shed a tear over a lost ship, or crew, especially a simulant crew. They'd only mourn the loss of equipment."

"I know my memory of them is pretty screwed up, but I don't remember the Hedalt having tear ducts."

"Very funny, Captain," said Sonner, though she was struggling to hide a smirk. "I'm glad to see your sense of humor has survived intact."

"Well, since I can't cry either, I guess I have no choice but to laugh," Taylor answered. "So, what do you think, do we try it or not?"

Sonner coughed and sank deeper into the chair. For a moment, Taylor thought she had nodded off. "One haggard Earth Fleet officer who feels half-dead already and a simulant with an overactive sentimental streak and a terrible sense of humor... we don't really have much more to lose, do we?"

"At least you still have a beating heart, Commander," said Taylor and then he did a double-take, "at least, I think you do anyway."

Sonner laughed and Taylor joined in, adding his own slightly artificial mirth to the harmony.

"Okay, Captain, it's a good plan, let's do it. I'll get the transceiver loaded onto a Nimrod, and then we'll head out and see who else is still out there in this miserable galaxy."

Taylor started to program the new course into the navigation computer, before replying, "Aye, aye, Commander Sarah Sonner."

NINETEEN

Taylor slowed the modified Hedalt Corvette to a hover in front of the tunnel that led back out to the moon's surface. Behind them, programmed to mimic Taylor's every maneuver, was a single Nimrod-class cruiser, loaded with the Hedalt transceiver that Sonner had removed from the Corvette back in the hangar. It was through this device that the ship had interfaced with the CoreNet, through the vast galactic network known as the Fabric. The transceiver was currently deactivated, but with a press of a button on Sonner's command chair, it would re-establish its connection to the CoreNet and give up the decoy ship's position. By then the Nimrod-class cruiser would be on an unstoppable collision course with the surface of the fourth planet in the system. This was hundreds of thousands of kilometers from the small moon where the Contingency base and Nimrod Fleet lay hidden inside a lava tube, protected from ship's scanners thanks to the unique composition of the volcanic crust. With the comms tower deactivated, it would take a miracle for a Hedalt scout to find the base, Sonner had argued. And if the Hedalt did send a recon vessel to the fourth planet they would simply discover the wreckage of a ship on the surface and move on. At the very least, it would draw the Hedalt's attention away from the moon. Taylor and Sonner both knew there were no guarantees, but it was the best they could do.

Taylor gripped the control column and let out a long slow breath as the tunnel entrance grew larger through his pilot's viewport. Then he laughed at the stupidity of what he'd just done; after all, he had no nerves to calm so taking a deep breath was utterly pointless. Sonner also appeared to have noticed his very human reaction to the challenging task ahead.

"Did you just sigh, Captain?" She asked the question as incredulously as if Taylor had just broken wind.

"Yes, and don't ask me why," Taylor replied, "though for some insane reason, it actually made me feel better to do it."

"Fascinating..." said Sonner, though for a change she wasn't being sarcastic. As an engineer, Taylor wasn't surprised that she would find the intricacies of his synthetic body intriguing. "You know, your simulant frame was something of an enigma to Earth Fleet's scientists."

Taylor glanced back, with an interested frown, "How so?"

"Compared to the rest of Hedalt technology – this old bucket, for example..." she said, gesturing to the ship around them, "the engineering complexity of the simulant frame was light years ahead. And we could never work out why they had gone to so much effort to make the bodies appear so real and organic. Take your simulated breathing as a prime example. It just seemed to be excessive and completely unnecessary."

"Maybe the idea of millions of stiff, walking, talking shop dummies freaked them out, and so they made them seem more real?" suggested Taylor, though he was being mildly facetious.

Sonner shrugged, "Who knows? But I for one am glad you don't look like some sort of early twentieth century sci-fi android, because that would certainly freak me out."

Taylor shook his head. Of all the people that should be freaked out, it was the man locked inside the simulant body. "Well, I'll try my robotic best not to offend you..."

"Appreciated, Captain," Sonner replied, missing the sarcasm. "Now, can you get us out of this damn cave, already?"

"Aye, aye, Commander Sarah Sonner," Taylor replied, before pressing his eyes back inside the pilot's viewport, and letting out another long breath. *Come on, Taylor, you can do this...* he said to himself as he encouraged the ship forward into the narrow mouth of the tunnel. Casey had made it seem so simple and now, more than ever, he wished that he had his quirky but brilliant pilot back in her seat, sequined sneakers and all. He didn't care if she was real or a simulant; she would still be Casey to him, and that's all that mattered.

The collision alarm sounded, gently at first and then increasingly louder as the hull of the ship came closer and closer to the side of the cave. Taylor adjusted course, grateful for the precision of his simulant hands for the first time since he'd seen the pale gray digits, and as the RCS thrusters inched them away from danger the alarms faded again.

"You're doing great, Taylor, just keep it going," said Sonner from behind him. He had been concentrating so intensely that he'd almost forgotten she was there.

He checked the distances displayed through the pilot's viewport, continually making minor course corrections, which became more frequent as the tunnel narrowed further. The dorsal alarm bleeped urgently, and a warning flashed up in his viewport, as the larger Nimrod in tow scuffed the rock of the tunnel. Taylor swore, but then overcompensated and sent the Nimrod scraping against the opposite wall instead. *Come on, get a grip!* he urged, as he teased both ships back into the center of the tunnel. The collision alarm rang again, and Taylor had to improvise; his trajectory through the tunnel had been thrown off by the impacts and associated corrections, and he was now headed directly for a cluster of jagged rocks that were jutting down from the top of the cave. He heard the sharp intake of breath from Sonner behind him as the collision alarm grew to a wail, but his steady simulant hands allowed him to steer the Corvette beneath the razor-sharp rocks and safely out into the hazy atmosphere of the moon. A few tense seconds later the Nimrod-class cruiser emerged too, still dutifully in tow, albeit slightly scraped and dented. He glanced behind and saw that Sonner's sickly pale skin had been supplemented with a new shade of green and he stifled a chuckle.

"No sweat," he said, noticing the beads of sweat on Sonner's brow. The lack of nerves in his simulant body meant that tense, nail-biting maneuvers, like piloting a huge space cruiser through a narrow rock tunnel, were a lot easier to perform. He had the steadiness of hand that a surgeon would kill for. Sonner, however, looked like a literal nervous wreck.

"I'm glad you think so," said Sonner as Taylor switched from thrusters to main engines and began the burn out of the moon's thin atmosphere and towards the fourth planet.

They continued to chat idly as the two ships surged towards their destination, but as the unremarkable planet grew close, they returned to the matter at hand, like the professionals they were. Taylor maneuvered the Corvette into orbit on the far side of the fourth planet, while Sonner prepared to remote pilot the Nimrod-class cruiser to its ultimate destruction on the surface.

"We're in position..." said Taylor, switching the main viewport to a display of the second ship. For some reason the sight of it made him feel a sense of melancholy. The vessel was not crewed, and so no-one would die, but the ship itself still had an identity, and it would still be sacrificed. To Taylor, it wasn't just a hulk of metal; it had been built to provide hope, a second chance to defeat the Hedalt and claim back Earth. That it would not get its opportunity to fight seemed sad and unjust, but though it would not be a participant in the war to come, if there was to be one, its demise still served a noble purpose. It would lead the Hedalt, should they come in search of their missing ship, away from the secret base that contained the very last hope for humanity to survive. It was a sacrifice, but a worthy one.

Sonner cleared her throat and announced the countdown. "Initiating crash program in three... two... one... initiate."

The thrusters on the Nimrod-class cruiser fired, angling its nose down towards the planet, and then the main engines lit up and burned brightly, propelling it rapidly out of sight.

"Enabling the Hedalt transceiver... now," Sonner added, once the ship was irrevocably committed to its suicidal trajectory.

Taylor adjusted the display on the viewport, tracking the ship and automatically increasing the magnification so that it remained clearly visible as it plummeted through the atmosphere, before crashing into the surface in a thick plume of brown-orange dust. The signal from the transceiver remained detectable, however, like an aircraft's black box from a time long-since passed.

"The signal is weak, but if a Hedalt ship does enter the system, it's likely they will find it," said Taylor, monitoring the transmission.

"Let's hope that's all they find," said Sonner.

Taylor nodded in agreement and then swiveled around to face the Commander. "So, where to now?"

"I've sent you the co-ordinates for the first of

the other two Contingency bases," said Sonner. "We start there."

Taylor heard his console bleep and glanced back to see the co-ordinates flash up on his screen. He swiveled the chair back and began to program the new coordinates into the jump computer. "It will take some time to plot this course and compute the series of jumps we need to make to get there," he called out.

"Whoa, hold up there, not so fast!" said Sonner, and then she pushed herself unsteadily out of the command chair. She hung over it for a moment, hands still attached to the arms, looking like she was about to fall back into it again. "It will require several jumps through the Fabric, before we can blind jump into what could potentially now be hostile space," Sonner continued, as she finally managed to stand unaided. "If the Hedalt have already found the other bases, I'm in no condition to go into battle. Hell, I feel like I could fall to pieces at any moment."

Taylor frowned, but withheld the urge to tell Sonner that she looked that way too. Instead he asked, "So what do we do now?"

"Now I go to bed, in the new quarters I've had built, courtesy of my little drone friends," said Sonner, "and, short of the ship breaking apart, a black hole opening up, or a fleet of Hedalt Corvettes jumping on top of us, I don't want to be woken for at least eight hours."

"And what the hell am I supposed to do for eight hours? Play tiddlywinks?"

"I suggest you get some sleep too. Your brain will need to rest, just the same as mine does."

Taylor held up his hands palms facing outward. "Woah, woah, you're not putting my head in that hole in the wall."

Sonner laughed, "Don't worry, I'll get one of the drones to do a hatchet job on the interface in your quarters, so that you can sleep on the table, with your head still on."

"Sounds cosy..." said Taylor, folding his arms across his chest.

"I'll sort you a proper bed out later, I promise, so it'll just be this one time," Sonner said as she ambled unsteadily towards the exit, looking as if she was ready to collapse. But as the door slid open she stopped, rested against the frame, and looked back at Taylor. "I know this is a crazy situation, and maybe it's crazier for us to go back out there, looking for trouble. But, you know what, I don't even feel afraid, and that's the most insane part of all this."

"I think that's just the fatigue talking," said Taylor. "Right now, I doubt you'd feel it if you walked straight into that door."

"No, that's not it, Taylor," Sonner continued, suddenly serious. Taylor couldn't help but notice she'd used his name, without his rank. "I just feel that somehow this was meant to be, you know? Like us meeting, and what happened to you, wasn't an accident."

"I've only been truly alive for less than a day, Commander," Taylor replied, "I honestly don't know what to believe."

Sonner smiled, "Then believe in me," she said, before stepping over the threshold of the door, "The chair is yours, Captain Taylor Ray. I'll message you when your own bed has been turned down."

"Be sure to leave a little chocolate on the pillow," Taylor called back, and he heard Sonner chuckle, before the door slid shut again and the bridge was plunged into silence.

Taylor rigged the ship for automatic running, before leaving the pilot's station and walking over to his old command chair. Dropping into the padded seat, it felt comfortingly familiar. He relaxed against the backrest and stared out at the lifeless planet and stars shining back at him through the main viewport. This was his home now; in fact the ship was the only home he'd ever truly known. Earth was a memory of another life; one that he had never lived. He thought of his crew and tried to picture their faces, though even so soon after their deaths he found it difficult to faithfully recall what any of them looked like.

Despite his body being artificial, his mind was real, and as fallible as any human's. Perhaps he did need to sleep, as Sonner had suggested, but he was also afraid of what he might see in his dreams, and how he would feel when he woke and was again confronted with what he was. *I guess there's only one way to find out.*

Taylor continued to stargaze until the panel in the command chair bleeped and he saw that a personal message had arrived from Sonner. 'Your bed has been prepared, Your Majesty. I couldn't find any chocolates. Sorry. See you in eight hours.'

Taylor snorted a laugh and then pushed himself out of the command chair. He took a last look at the dusty brown planet on the viewport, which was now home to a crashed Nimrod-class cruiser, and then headed back to his quarters. The strange contraption that had looked like an operating-table now had a series of additional wires crudely attached to it and leading into the head-shaped compartment above, making it look even more like a hideous torture device than before. There was a datapad resting on it and Taylor picked it up. On it was a simple hand-written message.

'Just lie down and shut your eyes, that's all there is to it. Don't let the bed bugs byte.'

Taylor smiled, appreciating Sonner's nerdy sense of humor, and set the datapad down.

"Okay, here goes nothing..." Taylor said, as he gingerly laid himself down on the table. He felt neither comfortable nor uncomfortable, and with a final, slow and utterly unnecessary exhalation of breath, he shut his silver eyes.

TWENTY

The deep space corridor stretched out in front of Taylor, as it had done the last time he'd appeared inside, surrounded by an unending sea of stars. It was peaceful and meditative, and he imagined that Casey would enjoy spending hours simply gazing out at the cosmos, but after several minutes of absolutely nothing happening, he began to have some reservations. *Simulants have pretty uninspiring dreams...* he thought, hoping that this wouldn't be the extent of his experiences while 'asleep'. He also hoped that simulants didn't experience the passage of time in this curious dream state in a one-to-one ratio with normal time, otherwise he was in for an incredibly dull eight hours.

He waited for what he guessed was probably another ten or fifteen minutes, and when nothing happened, he decided to walk along the corridor and see if he could find the starlight door again. Sure enough, the shining silver doorway soon appeared in front of him, but this time there was something different about it. As he got closer, he realized what it was – the door was open. He stopped and peered through the glowing silver frame, but on the other side there appeared to be nothing more than the same deep space corridor, as if he was looking into a mirror.

"Hello?" he shouted through the opening, "Is anyone there?"

There was no answer, and he felt foolish. *Of course there's no-one there...* Taylor scolded himself. *What was I expecting to happen? To be greeted by a simulant butler?*

Cautiously, he stepped through the opening, and as soon as he'd cleared the threshold the scene immediately changed. He was still surrounded by deep space, but in addition to the stars and galaxies there were also thousands of bright cubes of light, extending as far as he could see. They reminded him of the antique puzzle cubes that people used to play on Earth, except the little squares were hollow, rather than filled with color. The longer he peered out into space the more of these cubes started to appear, in the same way that staring up at the sky at night gradually reveals more stars. But unlike the stars, which were scattered in a chaotic pattern all around him, the organization of the wireframed cubes was not random. They formed an almost perfect grid, like a three-dimensional patchwork that extended throughout the galaxy. It was strangely beautiful, but also disorientating, and Taylor began to feel nauseous, reminding him of how he was again exposed to the full-range of physical feelings while inside the corridor.

He focused his eyes directly ahead, which seemed to settle his queasiness, and then walked forward a few more paces. As he moved, the arrangement of cubes seemed to shift around him, as if they were much closer than they appeared. He looked behind and the starlight door was still there, though unlike the cubes, its position had not changed relative to his, as if it had followed him, or Taylor had not actually moved at all.

"You would have loved to see this, Satomi," he said out loud, and the words just ebbed away into nothing. "Your scientific mind would have a field day trying to work out what this all represents!" Suddenly, the image of Satomi, dead in the room where Sonner had interrogated him, leapt to the front of his mind, and grief struck him like a hammer. He was utterly unprepared for the raw physicality of the pain and buckled to one knee, forcing his eyes shut in an attempt to press the memory out of his mind. But on top of the pain he was also angry – angry that he could only picture her as a lifeless simulant, not as the woman he knew. He didn't want to remember her that way. He wanted to remember her understated smile and her warm, comforting eyes. He wanted to remember how she always made him feel good about himself, simply by being there when he needed her. He wanted her back. *I promise, I will find you if I can, Satomi. I'll make it right for you, and the others too.*

Taylor opened his eyes and almost fell over; he was still in the same, ethereal corridor, but instead of deep space he was now suspended inside the lava tube. Looking down he could just make out the Contingency base, where he'd discovered Sonner, and where Casey, Blake and Satomi had been lost. He thought again of Satomi and he was suddenly accelerating towards the base at a speed that even a Nimrod-class cruiser couldn't hope to match, until he flowed through the walls of the base and back into the interrogation room, in front of Satomi's dead simulant frame.

"What the hell is going on?" he shouted into the room, but the words just receded into nothing. He knew he couldn't possibly be back on the base, yet it all appeared vividly lifelike, including the bodies of his crew.

"I don't want to see this again, take me away!" he yelled, as if he was issuing an order to whomever or whatever was controlling his transitions, but nothing happened. *Maybe I fell off that damned table and banged my head again, like in the hangar...* Taylor thought. Since he hadn't been able to will himself out of the room, he decided to leave the old fashioned way instead, and walked towards the door, but as he reached for the handle the scene changed again, and he was accelerated onto the deck of the hangar, directly in front of a collapsed and partially melted pile of containers. *This is where I fell...* he realized. He looked around the hangar and it appeared exactly as it had done just before he and Sonner had left, including the Nimrod-class cruiser that they'd taken in tow and crashed into the planet. *If that ship is still here then this must be a memory...* Taylor mused, *But I also can't physically be here either, can I?* Then he had a more sobering thought. *How do I get back?*

He remembered that everything had changed after he had stepped through the starlight door and pictured it again in his mind. Suddenly, his body rushed upwards, out of the hangar, through the thick rock that surrounded the lava tube and up into space, eventually moving so quickly that the starlight around him was just a blur of white lines. Then he was back in the corridor, surrounded by the matrix of wireframed puzzle cubes that seemed to divide up the galaxy around him. He dropped to his knees, dizzy from the extreme rate of travel, and gasping for breath as if he'd just run a hundred meter sprint.

After a few seconds the disorientation passed and he was able to stand again. He looked around, noting that instead of being in deep space he was now in a star system with a red sun, and was hanging above a dusty brown planet. He spotted something glinting nearby, reflecting the soft crimson glow of the star, and was again staggered by what he saw. *It's the Corvette. It's my ship!* He looked more closely at the scorpion-like shape of the Hedalt cruiser, noting the patches of repair work to the hull that had been conducted during its time on the Continency base. Then he realized something. *If this is my ship after we left, then this can't be a memory. This must be right now.* He was paralyzed by questions. Was this corridor simply allowing him to explore inside his own memories, he wondered. But he immediately discounted this option, since he couldn't possibly have a memory of his ship seen from his current viewpoint. *But if these are not memories, then what are they?* he asked himself. The answer that suggested itself seemed almost too fantastical to believe. *Am I actually travelling to these places in my mind?* It sounded ridiculous, but at the same time plausible. He was currently connected to the simulant apparatus in his quarters, which Sonner had mentioned provided a link to the other members of his crew. But perhaps the link extended further than this; perhaps his simulant-frame was wired directly into the CoreNet, and into the very Fabric itself. The CoreNet couldn't penetrate inside the Contingency base, which would explain why he only saw it as he remembered it before leaving, but outside of its volcanic shield, the CoreNet was everywhere. There was only one way to test to the theory, he realized, and that was to attempt to travel somewhere else; somewhere distant, but familiar. A suggestion immediately popped into his head – Earth. He had no idea what Earth looked like now, so if he was only exploring his memories, he'd see the planet as he remembered it, populated by billions of human beings and with Earth Fleet ships and outposts buzzing around it like bees.

"Why not? Earth is as good a place to start as any..." Taylor said out loud, and no sooner had the words escaped his lips, he was rushing through space towards one of the wireframed cubes at an incredible speed. The stars shifted all around him and soon he was inside the cube, hurtling towards its center, but he wasn't slowing down. He felt like screaming as an object at the center of the cube grew larger and larger, until it became clear that it was a planet. But the planet was not Earth. Then he rapidly changed direction and continued moving on a tangent to the first cube, speeding through space towards another one, getting faster and faster, until he changed direction again, towards a third. Breaking through the third cube's glowing framework, he changed direction again and again and again, so fast and so frequently that he started to black out. But, before his eyes darkened completely, the acceleration stopped as suddenly as it had begun. When the fog in his mind had cleared, Taylor discovered that he was on his hands and knees on the translucent floor of the deep space corridor. He was surprised to find that he was breathing heavily again, feeling the burn in his lungs. It didn't seem to matter that his body was merely a mental projection of his physical form; inside this place of thought and energy, everything felt real.

Once he had fully recovered, he stood up and looked around, but it didn't take long before he was confronted with something that again stole the breath from his lungs. "I don't believe it..." said Taylor in a hushed voice as it suddenly dawned on him where he was. "It actually worked!" He was near the center of one of the wireframed cubes, but now he was able to comprehend just how vast each one was, with each individual section engulfing what would have been hundreds of thousands of kilometers, maybe more. And in the very center, so close he felt like he could reach out and touch it, was a bright blue, cloud covered planet. From the shape of the continents there was no question that it was Earth, but Taylor knew it instinctively, like a baby recognizing the face of its mother. Yet, paradoxically, Taylor realized that this could well have been the first time his eyes had ever seen it. Either way, from his current distance, it was difficult to tell whether it was the Earth of his memory – the original Taylor Ray's memory – or the Earth of now. As he watched the planet slowly rotate, he became aware of something new and alien hanging in space close by; a black sphere, almost invisible against the darkness. At first he thought it was some sort of rogue asteroid, but then he made out the spikes protruding from the surface and realized what it was. *That's a super-luminal transceiver! The Hedalt must have placed one directly at Earth after the war.*

The presence of the super-liminal transceiver only strengthened Taylor's theory, but it was too early to make any solid conclusions. He would have to test the theory some more first, to see where else in the galaxy he could potentially travel. But, if it was true that he had unlocked an ability to traverse the very Fabric itself, it was a discovery that was not only simply astonishing, but one that could potentially give them a vital edge in the war to come.

TWENTY-ONE

The Hedalt War Frigate, commanded by Provost Adra, lurched out of the Fabric, having completed its blind jump to intercept racketeer raiders. Provost Adra took a reluctant, small step forward to help brace herself against the acute pain that had seized her body as a result of the jump. But she recovered swiftly and had straightened to her full height again within seconds. Adra inhaled deeply and let out the breath slowly, while adjusting her uniform, which was armored like a scorpion's exoskeleton, and long black coat to ensure her appearance was unchanged from how she had looked before the jump. This was not vanity – Adra cared not for such things – it was pride. Pride was something to be embraced; she was a Provost of Warfare Command, a member of the elite inner circle and the commander of one of the most powerful vessels in the Hedalt armada. She had attained her high status through ruthlessness, determination, dedication and raw ability. Anyone of lesser rank or status that looked upon her should know their inferiority and stand in fear and admiration.

Had her Adjutant been watching, he would have barely noticed Adra's discomfort, but as it was, Adjutant Lux was still holding tightly to the metal frames of the two pilot's chairs that bookended his station at the front of the bridge. Adra scowled; though her own pain was receding, it still felt like there were needles pressed into her eyeballs, yet she had shrugged it off, while Lux continued to show his vulnerability.

"Report, Adjutant Lux," said Adra, unwilling to allow her Adjutant the luxury of any more time to recover.

Lux released his hold on the chairs, which were occupied by two simulant pilots, and turned to face Adra, pressing his still throbbing hands behind his back to hide the fact they were trembling. "We have arrived at the designated system, Provost Adra," Lux began, using all his energy to control his voice to ensure the agony he was feeling was not apparent to his commander. "Scans are detecting two racketeer vessels and three freighters. One freighter has already been disabled and its cargo raided. The second and third are still under attack."

"Intercept the closest racketeer," Adra ordered, and then without waiting for Lux to reply, she pointed up to one of a halo of screens above her command deck and then drew her hand to her chest. The screen immediately swung down on a spindly metal arm and hung in front of Adra, displaying a tactical readout of the system. She studied it closely, noting that the two racketeer vessels were modified light cruisers, bastardized with weapons and upgraded engines no doubt stolen or salvaged from other victims of their acts of piracy. Adra clenched her teeth and her frown deepened. She hated racketeers; they were parasites that wasted their rare gift of being able to withstand super-luminal travel by preying on the supply lines in the farthest and least defended reaches of the empire. But no matter how insignificant the cargo in the greater scheme of the empire, Warfare Command would not permit even a single act of piracy to go unpunished. To do so would show weakness, and weakness repulsed Provost Adra, more than the racketeers themselves, and only slightly less than humans, whom she had helped make extinct.

Lux, meanwhile, had turned back to face the main viewport and rapped the back of his fist against the primary pilot simulant's shoulder, prompting it to begin a pursuit of the racketeers. The simulant automaton said nothing, but reacted instantly, powering up the powerful engines of the massive War Frigate and setting them on an intercept course. Lux then checked his own console, which showed a similar tactical readout to that of Adra's screen, and noted that the second freighter was also now in the process of being raided. He turned to face Adra to report the finding.

"Provost, the lead racketeer vessel has attached itself to the second freighter and is cutting through its hull," Lux began, "I suggest we adjust to intercept; there may still be time to prevent the loss of cargo."

Adra brushed her screen off to the side with the brusque mannerism of a Roman emperor dismissing a slave, and glowered down at Lux from the elevated position of her command deck. "Did I request your opinion?" she growled.

Adra's reaction caught Lux off guard. He had only recently become her adjutant, and though Adra's reputation preceded her, he knew nothing of her personality. "Apologies, Provost, I did not mean to presume..."

"You did not mean to, yet you did," Adra interrupted him. "You are not here to offer suggestions, Adjutant, you are here only to carry out my commands."

"Yes, Provost," Lux replied instantly, bowing his head slightly as he did so.

Adra pulled the screen back in front of her and then completed a short series of commands, before brushing it to the side again. "Follow the course I have indicated, and stand ready with all weapons."

Lux responded and turned back to look at his screen. He frowned, noting that the course Adra had programmed took them past the lead racketeer and its prey without slowing, and then on to the second. At the velocity she had indicated, there would be little-to-no chance of targeting the racketeer without risking damage to the freighter. He turned back, swallowing hard before asking the question. "Provost, the course indicated takes us past the lead racketeer..."

"Was my previous statement unclear, Adjutant Lux?" Adra cut across him again.

Lux bowed his head, "No, Provost. Apologies again." He then turned away and knocked the pilot simulant on the shoulder to initiate the course change. Unseen by him, Provost Adra continued to glower at his back for several seconds longer, before returning her attention to the screen, and locking weapons on the conjoined mass of the freighter and lead racketeer ship.

Before long, the War Frigate had caught up

with the lead racketeer, and as Adra had expected, it hastily began to detach. Greed was the principal weakness of all racketeers, and Adra also knew that the racketeer Captain would wait till the last moment to detach. But, her outlaw counterpart would have counted on the more powerful War Frigate decelerating first, so as not to overshoot, and since Adra had not done this, she had caught them with their hand still very much in the cookie jar.

"Fire forward cannons and turrets," Adra ordered, and the simulant at the tactical station to her right responded, silently carrying out the command.

Lux watched on, aghast, as a storm of plasma shards lit up the viewport and burst out into space. It was like the equivalent of firing a blunderbuss at a barn door, peppering not only the racketeer ship but also the freighter and the surrounding space. Both ships were hit multiple times and both exploded almost simultaneously, moments before the War Frigate surged through their flaming debris, bouncing fragments of scorched hull off its armor like a windshield deflecting bugs.

"Racketeer ship destroyed, Provost," Lux confirmed, though it did not need saying, "but the freighter was also destroyed." He expected Adra to acknowledge the destruction of the freighter as a mistake, or unintended collateral damage, but she did not.

"Continue on course," Adra ordered, as she targeted the second racketeer ship, which had broken off and was fleeing. "Maintain pursuit."

Lux knocked the pilot simulant, which responded by adjusting their course to intercept the remaining racketeer. As soon as he had done so, his console alerted him to an incoming message. It was from the fleeing racketeer. He read it and then relayed it to Provost Adra.

"The remaining racketeer signals that it wishes to surrender, Provost," said Lux. "It has powered down its weapons and is coming to a full stop."

Provost Adra did not answer, and instead merely monitored the time remaining until they intercepted. Since the Captain of the racketeer ship had chosen to reduce velocity and surrender, the gap between them was narrowing rapidly.

Lux waited patiently for a response, knowing that the racketeer had a right to a trial. Warfare Command preferred to parade criminal elements as a warning to others who would defy their authority, and though the outcome of the trials were a forgone conclusion, those who surrendered would at least keep their lives. But Adra continued to remain silent, and Lux chose not to speak up again, for fear of further displeasing his Provost.

Adra was, of course, also aware of the right to

trial, but she did not care for this rule. Her own position afforded her the ability to act unilaterally, within reason, and she had no intention of wasting any more time on this particular band of outlaws.

The pilot simulant reduced their velocity as the immense mass of the War Frigate approached the racketeer ship, like an eagle swooping down on a vole. Adra watched their distance to target fall to within weapons range and then looked up at her helpless prey on the main viewport.

"Fire all weapons," Adra commanded, again issuing the order in the direction of the tactical simulant, which obeyed without delay.

Lux's eyes widened and his mouth opened slightly with the intention of reiterating the racketeers' desire to surrender, but he caught himself just in time and remained silent, before turning to watch the shards of plasma annihilate the comparatively small pirate ship.

Adra watched Lux with interest, wondering if he would be foolish enough to point out Warfare Command's rules over surrenders, as if she herself would somehow not be aware of them. A more fateful mistake would be to question her actions, and become one of the many Adjutants in the centuries-long history of the Hedalt Empire to have been executed at the hands of his or her commander for disloyalty and dissent. But Lux remained silent.

Adra considered pushing him, to test the loyalty of her new adjutant further and to teach him a lesson, but these thoughts were interrupted by an alert from the halo of screens above her head. She peered up, noting that the alert had come from the screen that monitored activity in the CoreNet. She frowned and pointed to the screen, before drawing it down beside her. The alert indicated an unidentified, anomalous reading inside the CoreNet. All thoughts of Lux left her mind and she focused in on the data with a laser sharpness. An anomaly in the CoreNet was a serious event; the CoreNet carried everything from simple ship communications to the very control signals that maintained the entire simulant network across the galaxy. Any risk to the CoreNet was a risk to the very stability of the empire itself.

She pushed the screen to one side and fixed her intense green eyes on Lux again, noting that he had turned to face her already, seemingly aware of the danger. "Direct all resources to analyzing the signal anomaly," Adra called out, "ignore all other standing orders. This is now our sole priority." Then she paused, and with a darker edge added, "Is that understood, Adjutant Lux?"

The Adjutant bowed his head, "Yes, Provost Adra, it is understood." Then he set to work without another word.

TWENTY-TWO

The ramifications of his newfound ability to seemingly travel inside the Fabric were still bouncing around Taylor's thoughts when a bright flash of brilliant white light startled him. The light blinked out of existence and Taylor saw three ships, which had just emerged from a jump, close to the super-luminal transceiver that loomed just beyond Earth's orbit. Taylor didn't recognize the configuration of any of them, but two had the predatory profile of warships, albeit ships that were far larger than either a Nimrod or Corvette. However even these large cruisers were dwarfed by the hulking mass of the third vessel, which was like a giant stingray, soaring through the cosmos. Taylor had never seen anything like it, which must have meant that the original Taylor Ray had also never seen this class of ship before, or that it simply didn't exist at the time his brain was harvested. Whatever it was, simply watching it glide through space gave Taylor chills.

He knew it would be prudent to learn more about these new classes of Hedalt vessels, but he had an overwhelming itch to find out how else he could manipulate his newfound ability, and it was an itch he had to scratch.

"Satomi Rose, I know you're out there somewhere..." Taylor spoke into the void. He concentrated hard, trying to remember Satomi's face, the sound of her voice and how she moved; even how she smelled. He forced himself to remember the woman he knew, the Satomi from before his awakening, picturing her at her station on the bridge, rather than slumped in a chair in the Contingency base. He remembered one of their last moments on the ship, before discovering the base, when Satomi had stood in the threshold of his cabin door, and he had blown yet another opportunity to tell her how he felt.

"Show me where you are, Satomi, show me..."

And then he was moving again, away from Earth and back into the network of cubes dotted around the galaxy, jolting from one to the next until again everything became a blur. This time, his vision did fail. The jolting continued for several more seconds, as he travelled blindly through the cosmos, and then the sensation of movement stopped, and he could hear the thrum of a starship's engines. Next he heard voices, at first his own voice, followed soon after by Casey's, unmistakable in its joyfulness, like sonic sunshine to listen to, followed by a sarcastic quip from none other than Blake, right on cue. Then he heard Satomi, the frustration laced thickly through the tone of her reply, trying to put a stop to the seemingly endless frolicking of the pilot and TacSpec crew member.

"In case you two hadn't noticed, we are actually approaching the planet," said the voice of Satomi Rose. "So, perhaps you could pay attention to that, rather than whether Casey's hat is regulation issue or not."

"I'm just sayin', it ain't fair that she gets to wear a hat and I ain't allowed to," said the voice of Blake, though in classic Blake fashion, he wasn't really annoyed, he was just enjoying teasing Casey.

"No-one said you weren't allowed to wear a hat, Blake." This was his own voice, and hearing himself talk was a surreal experience.

"No, we just said you looked dumb in a hat, that's all..." said the voice of Casey, and though he couldn't see her, he knew how her eyes would have been smiling, and exactly how her lips would be curled up into a roguish smirk.

He continued to listen and as he did so his vision began to return, until he could see the bridge of a Nimrod-class cruiser, or the replica of it fitted to a Hedalt Corvette, the same as his ship. But it was not his ship, and these were not his crew. The differences were subtle for the most part, but to Taylor, who had memories of nearly four years with his version of Casey, Blake and Satomi, they were easy to spot. Some of it was down to simple changes, like how the bridge stations had been configured, right down to small details such as the level of screen brightness being far higher on Blake's second screen than the Blake he knew would have set himself. Then there were more obvious things, such as Casey's black bakerboy hat. He'd never seen Casey wearing anything like this, though he couldn't deny it suited her very well. But, though there were differences, after observing their interactions for several more minutes, he recognized them as the people he knew. Their characters were the same, tempered by different experiences, but sharing the same core memories and personalities that he and his Casey, Blake and Satomi shared. They all had the same brains, after all. It was good enough, Taylor thought. *It may not be my Satomi, or my Casey and Blake, but once they are woken up, they wouldn't stay the same anyway. At least they will know me; at least we'll have something in common.*

He peered through the main viewport, which was centered on a planet he didn't recognize, though there was no reason he should. This crew's DSR mission could be on the other side of the galaxy, for all he knew. Then he thought to see whether he could move closer to Casey's station and perhaps glimpse the co-ordinates on her screen, but as he stepped towards her, along his near-invisible tunnel, he could feel himself being pulled away. He stopped and felt a dull pain at the back of his head, which quickly began to build and become more intense. He stopped and rubbed the back of his neck. *What the hell? Where has this come from?* he wondered.

He tried to take another step towards Casey, but this time the pull away from her was even stronger. He found himself travelling again, accelerating through the hull of the ship and out of the unknown star system, until he was bouncing through the cosmic cubes again, travelling perhaps thousands of light years at super-luminal velocities until he stopped and found himself sprawled on his back in the corridor in deep space, feeling like he'd just been through the spin cycle in a laundry machine.

"Taylor, is that you?" said a voice. *Satomi's voice!* Taylor realized, feeling a sudden thrill. Taylor remained on his back, frozen. "Taylor, I don't know where I am, are you there?"

"Satomi?" said Taylor out loud, and this time his words lingered, rather than vanishing into the ether.

"I can hear you, but I can't see you. Where are you?" said Satomi.

"Satomi, is that really you?" Taylor was still too afraid to move, in case shifting position upset his connection to this version of Satomi, whoever and wherever she was. "Do you know who I am?"

There was a brief pause, "Of course I do, what sort of question is that?" she said, sounding exactly like the Satomi he knew. "But, *where* are you? I'm surrounded by darkness. I can see a hall or room ahead, but it's also dark. This feels like a dream, or a nightmare. I don't like it!"

"Do you know where you are, what system?" said Taylor, desperate to know if Satomi could give him her co-ordinates, or even a hint of where she was. "What's your mission?"

"My mission?" said Satomi, as if the idea of her being on a mission was completely alien. "I... don't have a mission. I've always been here, but I don't understand where here is. Taylor, what's happening? I remember you, like you've always been here with me. But, you're different now somehow. Please tell me what's going on, Taylor, I'm scared..."

"Satomi, listen to me," said Taylor urgently, "I don't know how long we've got, so I need you to tell me where you are. Tell me, so I can find you!"

There was no response and Taylor began to feel terror grip his mind. "Satomi!" he called out, again and again, but there was no reply. *No! I can't have lost her again! Not again!*

TWENTY-THREE

Taylor called out to Satomi again and again, willing her voice to return, but eventually he had to concede that she was gone. Shaken and mentally exhausted, he lay on his back in the deep space corridor and stared up at the stars for what felt like hours, until the strange stabbing sensation inside his head got worse, and forced him to get up. It was like a headache, but sharper – as if there was a shard of glass inside his brain, working its way deeper into the tissue. He looked around his new location properly for the first time; he was inside one of the cubes, close to an orange sun. Then his eyes caught sight of a shimmer of light, a reflection of the sunlight in something metal that was flying towards him. The shimmer grew quickly and became the clearly recognizable, angular shape of a Hedalt warship. It wasn't as titanic as the ship he'd seen at Earth, but it was far larger than its already sizable escorts had been. And compared to his own ship, it was a giant. If the Corvette was a scorpion then this ship was an eagle, but one that looked to have been chiseled from obsidian.

The pain in his head stabbed at him again and he squeezed his eyes closed; a human reaction, but one that curiously seemed to help. He opened his eyes again and staggered backward along the corridor. He was no longer in space, but inside a ship, perhaps even the ship he'd just seen flying towards him. He was on what appeared to be the bridge, though it was more than twice the size of the bridge of his own ship. On the bridge, at various stations, were simulant crew, each with blank, expressionless faces that he did not recognize. *Simulant automatons, perhaps?* he thought, remembering what Sonner had told him. He looked to the center of the bridge and saw two figures; one standing on an elevated central platform, surrounded by a ring of screens, high above, and the other at the front of the bridge, between two simulants. Both were dressed in what looked like light armor, similar to the protective clothing that motorcycle racers wore. The additional padding and protective shells only served to enhance their already tall and muscular physiques, making them appear intimidating, even from a distance. He moved closer to the figure in the center so that he could its face more clearly, and saw that 'it' was actually a 'she', with piercing green eyes and hair tied back tightly into a short ponytail. Then it struck him that he knew what she and her companion were. They were not human beings, despite their close resemblance to them, but Hedalt soldiers.

Taylor recalled Sonner's mention of how the Hedalt didn't actually look all that different to humans, though in his mind's eye he had still pictured them as looking somehow much more 'alien'. As it was, their appearance was almost anti-climactic. Other than their grayish, almost slate-colored skin they could easily pass for human, albeit humans with physiques that would make even Olympic track-and-field athletes jealous. The only other defining characteristic was that both wore expressions that suggested someone had called their mothers whores. A scowl was an expression that Taylor was comfortably familiar with; he often saw one staring back at him in the mirror, and far more often on the face of Satomi, but the Hedalt took looking pissed-off to a whole other level.

What the hell am I even doing here? Taylor asked himself, rhetorically. He hadn't been thinking about the Hedalt at the time, and even if he had been, his overactive imagination would have pictured them with bright red eyes or spikes growing out of their heads or with some other crazy appendage or feature. Anything other than simple gray-skinned humanoids that looked like they spent too much time in the gym.

He didn't need to ponder the question further, because the answer presented itself when the female Hedalt, perhaps the Captain, spoke. The language wasn't English, or any other Earth-based language Taylor recognized, but for some reason he could understand it all the same.

"The signal anomaly has reappeared?" said the female. Her tone was gruff and formal and she sounded distinctly peeved.

"Yes, Provost. The anomaly briefly vanished, but the signal has returned and is orders of magnitude stronger than before, as it is now centered on our location," said the second Hedalt, possibly a lieutenant or second in command. "It could simply be an error with our sensors, or merely a coincidence."

"I do not believe in coincidence," said the one who had been identified with the title 'Provost'; her scowl deepening further. "Analyze the data we have, but purge this anomaly from the CoreNet now. We cannot risk damage to the network."

The second Hedalt nodded, bowing slightly, and moved swiftly to a nearby station, where it issued orders to the simulant stationed there, seemingly by hitting it on the shoulder.

"Initiating purge now..." said the second Hedalt, and instantly Taylor felt the stabbing pain return inside his head, but with twice the intensity of last time, and with it there was a tingle, like the feeling of a low-voltage electric shock. He tried to back away, but the pain was growing too severe, and he couldn't concentrate. He pressed his hands to his temples, *Further away... Move further away!* Then he was back outside the ship, but the pain remained, only moderately diminished. He looked around trying to get a fix on a star constellation or nebula or something he might recognize, but he didn't even know where in the galaxy he was, and so it was like trying to find an atom in a haystack, never mind a needle. Then he saw a bright star, not only brighter than any of the others, but with an intensity that seemed out of place compared to the other pinpricks of light surrounding him. He concentrated on it, willing himself to travel to its location, and as the pain threatened to overwhelm him, he began to traverse the grid of cubes once again, bouncing from one to another like he was part of a cosmic pinball machine. Again, his eyes darkened until eventually everything was still and the pain in his head had numbed. He stood up, blinking rapidly in an attempt to trigger his sight to return, and then ahead of him he saw the starlight door frame. He ran towards it, but the pain and disorientation caused him to frequently stumble, until he eventually managed to pass through the opening where the pain suddenly vanished. He dropped to his hands and knees, still disorientated, and then lay down on his back with his eyes closed. His head was spinning, and for a moment he lost consciousness.

"Captain...Captain Taylor Ray...Taylor!"

He opened his eyes and he was back in his crew quarters, lying on the table staring up at the face of Commander Sarah Sonner.

"Hey, I thought I'd lost you then," she said, looking visibly relieved.

Taylor sat up and swung his legs over the side of the table. "What are you doing here?"

"Eight hours is up, sleepy head. What the hell was going on in that simulant skull of yours; it sounded like the mother of all nightmares?"

Taylor laughed, shook his head and smiled at her, "You have no idea..."

TWENTY-FOUR

The simulant worked in silence, adjusting the configuration of the purge transmission in an attempt to erase the anomalous signal that had destabilized the CoreNet, until the anomaly suddenly disappeared off its screen. It stopped working and sent a notification to the screen of Adjutant Lux, before facing its station again and remaining still, like a mannequin.

Lux saw the notification appear on his screen and moved over to the station, pushing the simulant aside as if it were simply an office chair that was in the way. "Provost, the anomaly is no longer present," said Lux.

Provost Adra stepped down from her command platform and moved over to the console, stopping just behind Lux. "The purge was successful?"

Adjutant Lux re-ran the analysis and then turned back to Provost Adra. "It is inconclusive, Provost. The anomaly has gone, but I am not certain that it was purged fully from the CoreNet."

Adra scowled and approached the console directly, barging the simulant further aside with considerably less subtlety than her Adjutant had demonstrated. The simulant staggered and fell, but then stood again and remained statuesque while Adra ran the analysis herself.

"Here," said Adra after a few seconds, and then she pointed to the screen. "The anomaly moved away through the Fabric, before the purge was completed."

Lux leaned in closer to the screen and peered at the information, "Apologies, Provost, you are correct," he said, surprised and also quietly embarrassed that he had not seen this himself. He turned to another simulant at a console nearby. "Trace the anomaly, I want to know where it originated." The simulant immediately set to work, without looking at Lux or even acknowledging the curtly-given order.

"A transmission anomaly like this could disrupt the transceiver network and threaten the integrity of the CoreNet; we must find the source," continued Lux, addressing Adra again, but Adra did not answer; she was still staring intently at the analysis on the console screen. Lux waited a moment, and tried again to get her attention. "Provost?"

"I heard you, Adjutant Lux," Adra replied, without taking her eyes of the screen. She valued patience; a virtue that her eager new Adjutant had yet to master. "Continue your analysis and locate the source. It is most likely to be a low-grade transport vessel, operating out of alignment, or one of the deeper Way Stations that has failed to properly maintain its transceiver array." Then she locked eyes with Lux and added, "But whoever is the cause must be found and punished."

"Yes, Provost," said Lux and he made to leave, but something about Adra's demeanor caused him to stop and turn back. "Does something else concern you, Provost Adra?"

Adra tapped a sequence of commands into the console and then stepped back into the center of the command platform. Above her, the halo of screens that surrounded the platform, each showing a different aspect of the ship's status of operation, all switched to display the very specific element of the anomaly's analysis that Adra had focused on. Adra craned her strong, elegant neck up to study the screens, while Lux waited next to the platform, careful not to step on it, perplexed by his commander's unusual behavior.

"Tell me, what do you see, Adjutant Lux?" queried Adra, as if she were a school master questioning a pupil.

Lux peered up and examined the information on the screens, which showed a series of animated 3D waveforms and a string of related data. He frowned, realizing he was being tested by his commander, likely as a result of his earlier mistake in not spotting that the anomaly had already moved away through the Fabric. This was an opportunity to redeem himself, but no matter how intensely he stared up at the screens, he did not comprehend what he was looking at, or why Adra considered it important. "I apologize again, Provost, but I am afraid I do not see anything significant."

Adra glanced down at Lux, who appeared sullen, and then returned her eyes to the screens, "Your background is in security, combat, tactics, correct?"

"That is correct, Provost."

"My background, as you are no doubt already aware, is science, engineering, intelligence," continued Adra. Lux was well aware of his commander's background, if only because it was so rare for those who served in the scientific or intelligence sub-services to attain the rank of Provost or the command of a War Frigate. Such roles were typically reserved for Warfare

Command officers with combat specialties, such as Lux. They had made an exception for Adra, largely on account of her aptitude and the significant role she had played in Hedalt history, but also because she had proved to be every bit as ruthless as the military Provosts of Warfare Command. "That is why I recognize this pattern, or at least, something very similar to it," Adra went on.

Lux's interest was piqued, but he was also grateful that his commander had not castigated him for his inability to answer. "What is it, Provost?"

"These patterns are similar to brainwaves," said Adra. "Human brainwaves."

Lux's shock at this answer was plainly written across his chiseled face. "Humans?"

"To be precise, they are the sort of patterns you might see from a high-functioning simulant," Adra continued, "such as those that crew our Hunter ships in the distant regions."

"I did not realize such ships still operated," said Lux, watching the patterns flow across the screens. He knew of the Hunter Corvettes and their purpose, but the last remnants of humankind that had fled Earth's destruction had been discovered and annihilated centuries ago. As such, he was surprised that any Hunter Corvettes were still in operation.

"Few remain, but they are still out there,"

Adra answered, and Lux detected a hint of resentment. "The High Provost considers them redundant, but if it were my choice, they would continue to search for another century or more; for as long as is necessary to be sure the humans are eradicated."

Adra broke away from staring at the screens and met the eyes of her subordinate, who was the only other non-simulant member of her crew. Most Hedalt could not survive the rigors of super-luminal jumps, which is why Hedalt warships were crewed mostly by simulants, plus one or two officers of Warfare Command. These elite soldiers possessed an exceptionally rare genetic mutation that proffered them with the mental and physical strength to endure space travel. But even for those who possessed the mutant resistance there were still significant dangers, with each jump taking a toll like a twelve-round boxing match.

"Any surviving human colony remains a threat," Adra went on, her tone emphatic. "Over time, as they multiply like insects, they will seek to enact vengeance upon us. They will never forget, and so, if necessary, we must turn over every stone in the galaxy to ensure they are exterminated."

Lux grunted his agreement, "Vengefulness is in their nature. But, surely they are all dead now?"

"Warfare Command believes so."

"But you do not, Provost?"

Adra pointed up to the screens. "These patterns are familiar, except that the frequency of these brain waves are higher than anything I've seen, even from the most complex simulants; they extend beyond even gamma waves."

Science talk was utterly lost on Lux, but he tried to contribute something nonetheless, "So, you are saying that a high-functioning simulant caused this anomaly? A Hunter simulant?"

Adra looked down at him and her eyes narrowed slightly. "That would be impossible," she said, and Lux looked crestfallen again, "Yet, we cannot deny the evidence. Whether it was a simulant or something else, the CoreNet was compromised, and whatever caused the anomaly is still out there."

"What does it mean?" asked Lux.

"I do not know," Adra replied, "but I do know that we must discover the source and its intent as a matter of utmost urgency."

"Surely, you do not mean to suggest the anomaly was caused deliberately?" replied Lux, finally catching up with Adra's train of thought. "Simulants think only what we tell them to think."

Adra was silent for a moment, studying the waveform on the screens, and pondering its possible meaning and implications. Simulants were all connected to and controlled through the CoreNet. The more basic automatons, such as those that crewed Adra's ship, had highly limited brain function, but the brains of the high-functioning Hunter simulants were intact. All thoughts were contained, boxed-off in a glass-house for their minds, encapsulated inside the vast network that was the CoreNet, but also shielded from it. If a simulant brain had somehow managed to shatter the glass and enter the Fabric, on a conscious or subconscious level, the implications could be catastrophic. The CoreNet linked everything together, through the Fabric; if the simulant control network was disrupted, simulants would cease to function and it would become impossible to operate their vast fleet of ships. On top of this, all super-luminal communications and data transmissions would be cut off. It would fracture the empire and throw it into chaos. Adra again stared up at the brain wave patterns showing on the halo of screens, and deep inside her, she knew it was more than just a random anomaly. But to be certain, she needed more information.

"I suggest nothing, Adjutant Lux," she said with a severity that caused Lux's head to bow lower, "but I rule out nothing, also. Now, find the source of the CoreNet anomaly and report your findings to me without delay."

Lux bowed lower and then promptly left to rejoin the simulants working on the deeper analysis of the signal anomaly.

"And, Adjutant Lux," Adra called out, after he had made it only a few paces away. Lux turned and stood to attention, looking up at his commander. "Careless mistakes will not be tolerated on this ship. Be sure not to make another."

Lux nodded and then turned, leaving Provost Adra alone on the command platform, deep in thought and with a growing sense of foreboding.

TWENTY-FIVE

Commander Sarah Sonner sat in the mess hall, which was a new addition to the ship's internal configuration courtesy of her army of repair drones, with an untouched cup of black coffee in front of her. She had listened to Taylor recount the events of his dream-like experience without a single interruption. When he had finished, she blew out a low whistle and then took a sip of the lukewarm coffee, causing her face to pucker.

"Damn it, Captain, you made my coffee go cold," complained Sonner.

Taylor's eyes widened, "Really, is that all you have to say?"

"No..." replied Sonner, huffily, "But I hate cold

coffee and I'm always grouchy until I've had at least two cups. Preferably two hot cups."

"I'm not sure I believe that you're ever not grouchy," Taylor hit back, "but I think we have more important matters to discuss than cold coffee, like what my dream or vision, or whatever the hell it was, actually means."

Sonner got up, moved over to the recently added food station, tipped the cold coffee into the recycler, and then placed the cup into the beverage dispenser. She punched the code for a black triple-shot Americano and waited for it to pour out.

"You know, it's a good job the Contingency base was stocked with enough food rations to feed a hundred and sixty for over three years," she said, picking up the coffee and taking a sip. She sighed contentedly, turned to face Taylor and then leaned with her back on the counter, "It just means all the more coffee for me."

"Sonner, I'm serious, stop messing around."

"I'm not messing around, I'm thinking," said Sonner, adopting a more thoughtful tone, "and coffee always helps me to think."

Taylor watched her take another sip of the hot, intensely dark beverage, and he realized he could actually smell it. He had never been much of a fan of coffee, but the smell only served as a bitter reminder that he no longer had a need or even an urge to eat or drink, because he no longer felt hungry or thirsty. He'd not considered the soothing and comforting aspects of food, though, or how isolating it might be to no longer need regular meals, when socializing and dining often went hand-in-hand. It didn't seem to matter right now, though, since the only other person he could socialize with was Sonner, and he could hardly avoid spending time in her company, whether he liked it or not.

"I think you can somehow travel through the Fabric," said Sonner, jabbing her coffee cup towards Taylor.

"If you had been listening, you'd know I already suggested that..." said Taylor, petulantly.

"And I'm agreeing with you," Sonner replied, with her usual prickliness. "I mean, it's the only logical conclusion. You were travelling through space at super-luminal speeds, moving from one pre-defined point to another. You even said you saw something that looked like a super-luminal transceiver."

"It was pretty far away from where I was, but I don't know what else it could have been; they're pretty distinctive," said Taylor, agreeing with Sonner's assessment. Then he had a thought, "But what about when I appeared on the Hedalt ship? There wasn't a transceiver nearby, not that I saw, anyway."

"Sure there was," said Sonner, undeterred by

Taylor's challenge. "There would have been a miniature one on the ship itself, communicating with the CoreNet, same as this ship. Only we ripped ours out and installed it onto the Nimrod we crashed on the planet, of course."

Taylor chewed this idea over for a few seconds. "I suppose that would explain why I couldn't get through the door the first time, when I was still on the base," he said, stroking his chin and half-expecting to feel stubble. "The CoreNet signal wasn't able to penetrate inside the lava tube; the volcanic rock acted like a shield. But out here, the CoreNet signal is all-pervading, and the ship's transceiver is still intact on the planet's surface too."

Sonner paused mid-slurp and pulled the cup away from her mouth. "What do you mean the first time?"

Taylor winced; his tiny little slip had tipped off Sonner to the fact he'd been hiding something from her. *Damn this simulant body; the least it could do is give me a better poker face.*

"I didn't tell you before because..." he paused, trying to work out how to put it.

"Because what?" said Sonner, looking and sounding offended.

"Because I wasn't sure if I could trust you at the time," Taylor blurted out. "Look, this has all happened pretty fast, and it's a lot to take in." Then he held up his plastic-looking hands and waved them at her, "And, in case you hadn't noticed, I've had other things weighing on my mind too."

Sonner scowled and took another gulp of coffee. "Fair enough, Captain," she said, with surprising coolness, considering how affronted she had been only moments earlier. "I guess you had no reason to trust me. But, bear in mind that I trusted you, despite what you were, and despite the fact you and your cronies were trying to kill me too."

Taylor hadn't considered this aspect. To Sonner, he must have seemed more terrifying than the monster-like creature the Hedalt had programmed his lab-grown brain to see, in place of a human woman. At least Taylor now saw Sonner for what she really was; Sonner still saw the simulant body that had been sent to hunt and destroy any surviving humans. To Sonner, he still looked like a monster.

"Point taken, Commander. I guess I've been pretty self-absorbed."

Sonner laughed. "I don't blame you, Captain. But, from now on, no more secrets, agreed?"

Taylor nodded. "Agreed, Commander."

"So, you were saying about this first time?"

Taylor explained about how he'd first appeared in the ethereal corridor in space after falling from the stack of containers, and how at the time he couldn't get though the starlight door. But then how once they were outside the lava tube and exposed to the signals that traversed the Fabric, the door appeared to open and allow him through.

"And there's another thing..." said Taylor, hesitant to add the detail about Satomi, but unwilling to immediately break his promise to not keep secrets.

Sonner's right eyebrow lifted slightly. "Go on..."

"I talked with Satomi. Satomi Rose, from my crew," said Taylor, realizing how fanciful what he'd just said sounded when spoken out loud.

Sonner chewed the inside of her mouth, holding her coffee cup just in front of her chin. The memory of shooting the Satomi simulant was still fresh in her mind. "Presumably, you don't mean the actual Satomi from your crew, because..."

"No, not her," Taylor was quick to interrupt, before Sonner could say, 'because she's dead' or words to that effect. He didn't want reminding of that fact, or that it was Sonner that had shot her. Though he now realized that his sadness and angst over Satomi's death had diminished enormously knowing that she was still out there, in one form or another. He knew that the Satomi he'd spoken with wasn't the same, but in many ways she was, and the more he thought about it, the less this mattered to him. "It was a different Satomi," clarified Taylor. "I don't know where she was, because I could only hear her, not see her, but she sounded different."

"Different how?"

"Different like me. Like she was awake, or at least more self-aware."

Sonner wrinkled her nose and sniffed, and then turned back to the beverage dispenser to top up her cup with another two shots.

"Go easy with that stuff, or that sleep you just had will be your last for a week." Taylor had made the comment jovially, with the intention of lightning the mood, which had suddenly become tense, but Sonner did not oblige.

"Look, Captain, I know that finding your crew is important," Sonner said, turning back to face Taylor, freshly topped-up coffee cup steaming in her hands, "but you shouldn't get your hopes up."

"I'm not naïve, I know there are no guarantees of finding her," Taylor replied, unwilling to entertain a reality check; he was on a high and wanted to ride it for as long as possible.

Sonner sipped the coffee and then sighed, "It could just have been a dream, or your imagination. You could just have seen and heard what you wanted to see and hear."

"I don't believe that."

"Well, you wouldn't, would you?" said Sonner, who had run out of patience with the tactful approach. "You've just lost everything, and you'll do anything to cling on to a part of that past. I understand you wanting to grasp hold of something that connects you back to them, but be careful you don't hinge all your hopes on it. Because you may never find them."

"Damn it, Sonner, were you always such a bundle of joy?" said Taylor, stalwartly refusing to let Sonner drag him down.

"I'm just being real, is all."

"Well, my definition of reality has been redefined of late, in case you hadn't noticed," countered Taylor. "So I'm choosing to believe they're out there – that *she's* out there – and that's that."

Sonner raised the cup to her lips and then drained the contents, before letting out a contented sigh. "As you wish, Captain." Then her expression seemed to brighten. "Besides, if what you're saying is true then we can use it to our advantage. It could help us stay ahead of the Hedalt. It can help us locate the bases and plan the jumps to avoid heavily guarded areas."

Once again, Taylor couldn't argue with Sonner's logic. There was no doubt that it could be a great tactical advantage – but that wasn't the application of this ability that he was most interested in exploiting. "And it also means that we can locate the Hunter ships and find my crew,"

Taylor added, plainly.

Sonner observed Taylor for a few seconds, noting how the artificial muscles in his face had relaxed at the mention of finding his crew, exactly as they would have done if he was still human.

"I agreed to help find and wake up your crew, Captain, and I'll be true to my word."

"But..." Taylor added, before Sonner had a chance to say it. This appeared to irritate her.

"But, the mission has to come first. There's no point saving your crew if we can't put the Contingency into action and take the fight back to the Hedalt."

Taylor knew the mission had to be the priority, but he still had to be sure that Sonner would honor her word, as she claimed.

"So long as you promise me," Taylor said, with a chilling seriousness that could have frozen the coffee in Sonner's cup, had she not already drunk it. "Promise on your life, your honor, mother, cat, dog, whatever, I don't care. But as long as you promise me, I'll agree."

Sonner thought about this for a moment. "Okay, Captain Taylor Ray, I promise on the life of my brother, James Sonner, that I will help to rescue your crew, if they're out there."

This took Taylor by surprise; he wasn't expecting to extract some personal information from her; in fact, he'd never even considered asking about her personal life. Had she been married? Children? The thought of what she might have already lost was disquieting and he realized how selfish he'd been.

"I'm sorry, Commander, I hadn't even thought to ask if you had family."

Sonner sucked her bottom lip, mulling over how much to reveal and which details to elaborate on, and then said, "He was stationed on one of the other Contingency bases. I cashed in all my favors to get him there." Then her lips pressed more tightly together, before adding, "He could be dead. For all I know, he probably is. But, until I know for sure, that's the most solemn vow you'll get from me."

"In that case I accept," said Taylor. He didn't want to push her to reveal anything further; clearly even revealing this much had been tough.

Sonner nodded and smiled. "At some point, I'll need to take a look at your head..." Taylor recoiled. "Still attached to your neck, of course..." Sonner added quickly, "in order to figure out what happened to wake you up. If I can figure that out then perhaps I can devise a way to wake up the others too."

"Thank you, Commander," said Taylor, and there was genuine warmth in his simulated voice that made Sonner seem to glow.

"But, first, I have to go and make your bed,

literally, before we jump out into the unknown."

Sonner placed the coffee cup down on the counter and started towards the door, which she had actually had widened into an open archway. But before she'd made it all the way through, Taylor called out, "Don't forget the little chocolate on my pillow this time!"

"Screw you, Captain..." came the playful reply as Sonner disappeared though the exit, boots thudding down the corridor away from the bridge.

TWENTY-SIX

Taylor waited in the mess hall until Sonner's footsteps had faded completely and then got up and made his way to the bridge. Their course was already set, but he still wanted to double-check the computations and get ready for their first blind jump, back to the closest super-luminal transceiver. From there, they would traverse half-way across the galaxy, in search of the last remnants of human civilization; if any remained alive. As he entered the bridge he paused for a moment, glancing at the three empty stations, and picturing Satomi, Casey and Blake at work. The bridge seemed so cold and cheerless without them, and also a lot bigger.

He slid down into the pilot's chair and

verified the jump settings, before running the numbers again, just to be sure, since it was usually Casey that did this. But everything checked out; they were ready. *Ready?* Taylor thought. *Ready for what? One ship and two crew against a galaxy full of Hedalt, all bent on our destruction.* The more he thought about it, the more it became apparent how hilariously not ready they really were. But, perhaps in some strange way this gave them an advantage. An armada was easier to spot, easier to fight; one little ship was like a drop of ink in an ocean. But, despite all that had happened, and regardless of the hardships they yet faced, Taylor was determined to go forward, and embrace his new existence.

"We know what we are, but know not what we may be..." Taylor spoke out loud, doing his best to sound theatrical. He then instinctively looked over to the TacSpec console, expecting Blake to complain about him quoting Dickens or Hemingway or King, or whichever incorrect author he would attribute the quote to in an effort to bait Satomi into responding; which, of course, she always did.

His thoughts dwelled on them again. Their four years together, or however long it had actually been in real terms, had connected them profoundly, in a uniquely human way. It was true that the Hedalt could shape their perception of the world, but Taylor had to believe that authentic human connection was something that exceeded their power of influence. The experiences and memories they had all shared may not have all been real, in a physical sense, but they were still real to him. The bonds they had formed were true. He closed his eyes and spoke their names out loud.

"Blake Meade. Casey Valera. Satomi Rose. I promise I will find you again. I promise that I will find you and that I will wake you all. I'll give you a chance to see what I see, and to be the people you were meant to be."

He opened his eyes and then picked up his datapad, which was resting on the console in front of him. He logged into his personal account and then stopped. *No, that person isn't me, not anymore.* He logged out again and created a new account under the name 'Taylor Ray – Awake'. He moved to the journal section and opened a blank page. For some time he simply sat back in the pilot's chair and stared out of the viewport at the millions of stars in front of him, letting his mind roam freely, the same as Casey had often done. Then he peered down at the datapad and began his entry.

Personal Journal – Entry #1

My name is Taylor Ray and I am awake. I don't know yet who I really am. The real Captain Taylor Ray died over three hundred years ago, so I know I'm not him, but I also know that a part of me is.

Which part, I can't be certain, but it no longer matters. I am not him. I am somebody new.

What I do know for certain is that the only things that were ever real to me were my crew. My family. I know they are still out there somewhere. They don't know who they are yet either, because they are not awake, and they sure as hell don't know me. Not the new me. But I'm going to find them, and I'm going to free them. I'm going to wake them up to the reality I now know. That is my mission, for as long as this simulant body can carry me. And then, perhaps one day, when the Hedalt have been routed and the victory won, we can all return to Earth and together we can see it for the first time. As a family. Maybe that apartment overlooking the Colombia river is still there, who knows? But if it's not, we'll build it again.

Above all, I want Satomi to see what I see. It's beautiful and terrifying, but it's real. One day we'll gaze upon the galaxy of stars together, with newborn eyes and a head full of dreams.

The end.

TO BE CONTINUED...

The Contingency War Series continues in book two, The Way Station Gambit.

The Way Station Gambit:

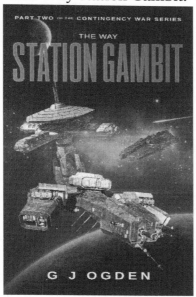

All the books in the series:

- **The Contingency**
- **The Way Station Gambit**
- **Rise of Nimrod Fleet**
- **Earth's Last War**

ALSO BY THIS AUTHOR

If you enjoyed this book, please consider reading The Planetsider Trilogy, also by G J Ogden, available from Amazon and free to read for Kindle Unlimited subscribers.

The Planetsider Trilogy:
A post-apocalyptic thriller with a military Sci-Fi twist

- The Planetsider
- The Second Fall
- The Last of the Firsts

*"The strong action sequences and thoughtful worldbuilding make this one worth picking up for fans of plot-driven SF." - **Publishers Weekly***

ABOUT THE AUTHOR

At school I was asked to write down the jobs I wanted to do as a 'grown up'. Number one was astronaut and number two was a PC games journalist. I only managed to achieve one of those goals (I'll let you guess which), but these two very different career options still neatly sum up my lifelong interests in science, space and the unknown.

School also steered me in the direction of a science-focused education over literature and writing, which influenced my decision to study physics at Manchester University. What this degree taught me is that I didn't like studying physics and instead enjoyed writing, which is why you're reading this book! The lesson? School can't tell you who you are.

When not writing, I enjoy spending time with my family, walking in the British countryside, and indulging in as much Sci-Fi as possible.

You can connect with me here:
https://twitter.com/GJ_Ogden
https://www.facebook.com/TheContingencyWar

Subscribe to my newsletter:
http://subscribe.ogdenmedia.net

Made in the USA
Lexington, KY
13 November 2019